Riley w...
"That was despicable!"

Nevertheless her feelings whirled in confusion around anger and a strange regret that his disturbing kiss had ended.

Freyn merely shook his head. "I don't understand. You enjoyed being kissed, but you won't admit it, even to yourself. You enjoy my company, but you won't admit that, either. If I didn't know better, I'd think you didn't like me at all."

"If you weren't such an egotistical brute, you'd understand it perfectly," Riley retorted.

"You're not angry with me, Riley Jones," Freyn remarked. "You're angry with yourself because you're feeling trapped. You didn't really mind being kissed. You just can't stand it when you're not totally in control, can you?"

Damn him, thought Riley—for being able to play on her emotions with such skill and for knowing her all too well.

Victoria Gordon, one of our leading authors from the "land down under," has charmed Harlequin Romance readers for several years with her humorous, engaging style. Her characterizations are evocative and her storylines always stimulating. Many of her books are set in the Australia she knows and loves.

Books by Victoria Gordon

Forest Fever

Victoria Gordon

Harlequin Books

TORONTO • NEW YORK • LONDON
AMSTERDAM • PARIS • SYDNEY • HAMBURG
STOCKHOLM • ATHENS • TOKYO • MILAN

Original hardcover edition published in 1986
by Mills & Boon Limited

ISBN 0-373-02854-7

Harlequin Romance first edition August 1987

CHAPTER ONE

RILEY Jones strode angrily along the fifth-level ramp of Hobart's Centrepoint car park, moving in long strides that made her high heels clatter on the cement in loud accompaniment to her muttered curses.

Her feet, unaccustomed to the high heels, ached and throbbed. But her mind was in far more pain as it writhed in the torment of frustration.

Damn the man anyway! Damn all bankers—but especially the smooth, smarmy, sanctimonious one she had just left.

'And damn your children, too,' she muttered aloud as she reached the spot where her battered old four-wheel-drive utility squatted on sagging springs. 'Not that I think you'd be man enough to have any!'

As she gingerly slid herself into the truck seat, carefully arranging the skirt of her tailored business suit, she sighed heavily, thinking that she really ought to have accepted the omens of the early morning and postponed her appointment to another day.

It had been that sort of day right from the start. She had spent a restless night, finally getting to sleep in the early hours, then had overslept, waking only partially to the demanding ring of her telephone.

Riley had understood the message from the banker's secretary, but had been too sleepy to object to having her appointment changed from mid-afternoon to nine-thirty that very morning. Only after hanging up did she realise the time factors involved, and by then it was too late. Besides, having spent most of the night psyching herself up for the confrontation, she just couldn't face putting it off any longer.

The quickest of showers, complete with a ritual washing of her short-cut dark hair, had been followed by a fortunately easy decision about what to wear for this most important meeting. Riley only owned one outfit that she considered really suitable.

'Always look as prosperous as you can when you're asking to borrow money,' her father had always said. And Iain Jones should have known—he'd been an accomplished borrower during his lifetime!

'Bank managers are conservative types. They have to be,' he had once said. 'There's no room for imagination when you're handling other people's money.'

Which was why his single good business suit had only been worn for bank visitations and funerals. The final occasion had been to his own funeral just a month earlier.

She had paused to look in the hall mirror before leaving her small cottage, and grinned wryly at the image that returned the grin. What she saw was a slender figure wearing a crisp white blouse beneath a dark navy skirt and blazer combination that to Riley's eye fairly shrieked of a businesslike attitude. Sheer tights revealed shapely legs and feet tucked into dark navy shoes that gleamed with polish.

'I look like somebody's private secretary,' she had remarked to the mirror. 'Hair just right, make-up properly conservative. All I need now is a briefcase.'

The mirror-image mouthed silent replies, but couldn't explain the relevance of her appearance as it applied to getting carry-on finance to keep her logging outfit—and her future—from being sold out from under her! Her father's death, and the fast deterioration of his cancer-ridden body before the merciful release of death, had left Riley a very questionable legacy indeed.

She had given up her forestry studies only months

before graduation to nurse her father through the terminal stages of his illness, ignoring his protests that she might never be able to afford to return to university.

'I'll manage when the time comes,' she had replied, and never for an instant regretted the decision, not even when the small, wiry logging contractor had died before the graduation ceremonies she hadn't attended.

His estate comprised the small cottage at Orielton, a village on the Tasman Highway between Hobart and the east coast of Tasmania, plus a log skidder, an ageing Allis Chalmers HD11 bulldozer and an even older International log truck and jinker. Only the cottage was paid for. Along with Riley's battered and worn-out Suzuki utility. Everything else was heavily mortgaged, a serious situation indeed at a time when a flagging economy would mean shocking losses if she was forced to sell off the equipment now. But could she convince a banker she had never met to help her put the operation even further in debt? Riley didn't know, and didn't dare ponder the question too deeply. She could only try.

'And it isn't going to help if I'm late for the appointment,' she had muttered to herself as she picked her way along the rough driveway to where the utility sulked in a makeshift shed. On a bench beside the vehicle was yet another bad omen—the new tailshaft she had planned to fit this morning before leaving on her trip to the city.

The universal joints in the old truck were shrieking their last gasp, but only late the night before had she finally taken delivery of the required parts to effect repairs. Because of the particular model, she had the easier but more costly job of replacing the entire tailshaft instead of just the U-joints, but even that would take time.

Today there had been no longer time to spare.

'Well, old mate. We'll just have to take it very, very

gently and hope for the best,' she had sighed, absently patting the truck's faded mudguard as if it were the shoulder of some patient horse.

The truck's battered outward appearance belied the tidy interior, the result of considerable labour on Riley's part the day before as she had waited and waited for the repair parts that didn't arrive until well after dark.

As the engine grudgingly rumbled to life, she had the irrelevant thought that she might have somehow offended the poor old truck with such a thorough cleaning job.

'Probably the first time you've been this clean inside since you came out of the showroom,' she said as she carefully backed out of the yard and drove gently towards the highway.

She could feel the vibration in the drive-train. The worn U-joints screamed as if in pain and every change of gears resulted in a menacing, unhealthy *clunk* as the loose system shuddered under the strain.

'I must be mad!' she cried aloud as the truck finally settled into fourth gear and laboured into the thirty-five-kilometre journey ahead.

Throughout the trip, Riley had maintained as steady a pace as possible to minimise the strain, alternately praying for the truck and cursing other road-users when they forced her into gear changes she might otherwise had avoided. She had reviewed the arguments she was to present to the bank manager—arguments that must be accepted if she didn't want to be locked into a forced-sale situation that could only mean financial disaster from her viewpoint.

She knew her business—knew it perhaps more intimately than had her father, given the advantage of her education. And she could do the work, although convincing the banker of that might not be so easy! She had grown up with logging equipment, and by her early teens she had been driving bulldozers and skidders, using a chainsaw and axe, and capable of any job that a boy her age could handle. She had put herself through university on money gained cutting railway sleepers, working through weekends and vacations with an ageing bush mill and a borrowed tractor.

Riley and Bill Gunn, the son of the independent sawmill operator who provided her father with most of his work, had made a formidable team in the bush— until that final vacation when Bill had suddenly begun wanting more than just teamwork. He had wanted a wife, and while it wasn't surprising to Riley that he thought she should agree, it certainly didn't fit in with her own plans at all.

'You don't want a wife; you just want a free mechanic!' she had replied laughingly to his first proposal.

But he hadn't laughed in response.

'I'm serious, Riley,' he had said, and for the next three weeks took every opportunity to press his suit.

Riley was not impressed. It wasn't that she didn't like Bill. She did. But she certainly didn't love him, nor did she believe for one minute that he loved her, either. Trying to get that message across had proved harder work for Riley than the dawn-to-dark work of cutting the dense blue gums and manhandling them through the mill to create the heavy railway sleepers.

She had at first tried to do it gently, but during the three weeks Bill had become more and more insistent and her own objections to his proposal replied by becoming more and more blunt.

'I don't love you and I won't marry you. Final!'

'But *I* love *you*,' he had replied, as if that were all that was required.

'You don't know what the word means,' Riley had snapped, angered by his refusal to see sense. 'Just because we make a good team in the bush and we grew up together and have similar interests it doesn't mean we're in love!'

It had been a difficult argument, not least because she knew both her father and Julius Gunn had virtually taken it for granted that she and Bill *would* marry.

'I don't see how you can reckon to be any expert on the subject,' Bill had replied. A bit peevishly, she thought. 'Or is there somebody I don't know about?'

'Only if you call a forestry degree somebody,' she had cried, allowing her frustration to boil over. 'Leave it, Bill. This is a stupid argument and I don't want it to go on. I am positively sick and tired of the subject!'

'You'd come to love me!'

And just the way he said it, so smugly and with such blithe unconcern for her own feelings, made Riley realise that coming to love Bill would be the last thing she'd do.

'I'd come to hate you!' she had replied bitterly. And walked away without hearing his response. Not caring.

That had been her last day of working with Bill. She had walked away from him and kept walking until she reached her truck, then she had driven home with the road blurred because of tears she didn't quite understand.

A few days later, the first signs of her father's cancer had struck at her life like a bombshell, and the issue of marriage, to Bill or anyone else, had been lost in more important considerations.

But, since the funeral, Bill had quietly been making his presence known, and she sensed that the issue of marriage was once again in his mind, though farther from her own than ever. Riley's mind was occupied with just one thing—trying to hold together her father's business long enough for prices to return to normal—or at least reasonable—levels so that she could find the finances to finish her schooling. And the only way she could see to manage that was to take the machinery to the forest and put it to work.

She had hoped to have firm contracts to lay before the banker, but the past three weeks had given her only a few days' work at a time. Enough to keep food on the table, but not enough to service her debts.

When she entered the banker's plush office, it took only an instant for her to realise that it didn't matter anyway. Even given long-term contracts, this man wasn't going to help her, because what she proposed was to work in an industry that was traditionally a male preserve—and because this sleek, well-fed creature in his tailored suit was a worse chauvinist than she had ever encountered in any logging camp. From the instant he had emerged into the customer service area to greet her, she had felt the man's eyes crudely undressing her, and had been forced to choke down a taste of revulsion at his entire attitude.

Riley wasn't unaccustomed to masculine attention. She was, she knew, a relatively pretty girl with a healthy, shapely figure. She had grown up with the rough, direct sexuality of loggers and truck drivers, and learned the more sophisticated attitudes of city men while at school.

Personally, she preferred the loggers, to whom a lady was a lady until she proved otherwise. Their directness was easily managed and inevitably open and forthright. This man was anything but!

He was dealing from a position of power and he knew it. He used the knowledge, and was used to using it. Riley found herself wondering how many pretty young bank clerks had found their jobs hinging on compliance to his non-vocational wishes. He was, she realised, probably younger than her father had been, but he looked soft, somehow less than totally masculine. There

were no hard edges about him, only a faint aura of
expensive cologne designed to stir the emotions of his
office girls.

He smelled like a peat bog, Riley decided, and was
offended by the deception. This man had probably
never so much as seen a peat bog, and certainly had
never got those delicately-manicured fingers into
anything dirtier than his own ledgers! She had shaken
his flaccid hand, met shifty eyes with her own clear,
blue-grey gaze, and known instinctively that her
father's advice was wasted here.

Half an hour later she had left his office so tight-
lipped with anger and frustration that she could hardly
speak. And only just in time; one more sexual innuendo
or patronising remark and she would have exploded!
She felt like she needed a bath!

Now, as she savagely twisted the truck's ignition key,
all that anger seemed to solidify. When the vehicle
surged into life, Riley slammed it into reverse, backed
hurriedly from her parking bay, then threw it into the
lowest forward gear and dumped the clutch as she
trampled angrily on the accelerator.

Stupid!

There was a great shuddering, a tearing, clanging
sound from beneath her seat, and she realised with
sudden horror that she had just destroyed the worn
universal joint she had so carefully nurtured all the way
to town. Stunned by the result of her stupidity, she sat
for an instant, unhearing, unseeing. Then she frantically jammed her foot on the brake as she realised the truck
was rolling backwards toward a collision.

Riley managed to get the parking brake locked, only
a whisker from destroying the tail lights of the
expensive station sedan behind her, then sat for a long
moment in silent communion at her good luck in not

hitting the car. With shaking fingers she switched off the ignition.

She closed her eyes and fought for control. Moments that seemed like hours sped by as she heaved deep sobs and waited for her body to stop shuddering. Then she got out.

Kneeling beside the truck, she saw exactly what she could expect to see—the now disengaged tailshaft dangling from the remaining universal joint. Its position was such that she couldn't even move the truck without first getting that damaged part out of the way.

She sighed. There was no way out of this except to get out and get under. Once she had the wrecked tailshaft out of the way, she could limp home, however slowly, using the front half of the four-wheel-drive system.

'And no sense whingeing about it, either,' she growled to herself, rising to fling open the truck door and beginning to assemble her collection of spanners and the several clean feed-sacks she habitually carried for just such emergencies. Keeping the old truck on the road had been increasingly difficult since her father's illness. It was old and worn, and prone to crankiness at times. And without the money for regular servicing . . . She ought to have replaced the universal joints months ago, but just couldn't manage to.

Two minutes later, Riley was prone beneath the truck, her skirt rucked up around her thighs and her face running with perspiration as she struggled to free a stubborn bolt. Her suit jacket was inside the vehicle, and she had already accepted the likely ruination of her blouse. That thought did little for her temper, and when she barked her knuckles for the fifteenth time, she let loose a stream of invective usually reserved for recalcitrant bulldozers.

It was language historically linked to the days when bullock teams were used in the forests, and it mingled incongruous combinations of colourful profanity.

'Do you really think that's going to help?'

The voice, while soft-spoken enough, fairly dripped with a sarcasm that only served to heighten Riley's anger. And when she twisted to see a pair of ultra-shiny dress shoes only inches from her too-exposed thighs, she didn't bother to soften her reply.

'What business is it of yours?' she snarled, reaching down with greasy hands to try to straighten her skirt without ruining it along with her blouse.

'None, I suppose. I just couldn't help being impressed by the vocabulary, that's all!'

The shoes didn't move, and Riley could almost feel the man caressing her legs with his eyes. 'Do you habitually talk to your vehicles like that?'

'That,' she replied acidly, 'is none of your business either. So unless you're waiting to see how I talk to you, why not just push off? I'm a bit busy for idle conversation or stupid questions right now, in case you hadn't noticed.'

And again she was conscious of his unseen eyes, though the attention only served to make her even more angry. Riley was in no mood to be intimidated, especially not while she was in such a defenceless position. Not after what she had been through with the bank manager, whom she fully intended to change at the first opportunity.

'I'd love to oblige, but it's going to be difficult, the way you have my car boxed in,' was the cool reply.

'Yes, well, I'm sorry about that. I'm working as fast as I can, or at least I was until you started interrupting,' Riley replied in a cutting voice—then stifled another curse as she once again scraped her knuckles. 'Why don't you go and have a coffee or something? I won't be long.'

No reply, but the silence fairly screamed.

And the shoes didn't move. Nor did the intensity of his interest in the view she presented seem to decline.

It was all too much!

Riley reached out to grab at the edge of the truck and lever herself out from underneath.

'That's much better. I usually like to see who I'm talking to!' And strong fingers wrapped round her wrist before she was bodily lifted upright to balance on one foot as she peered up at the stranger.

Hazel eyes met her own from a height well above her diminutive five-foot-four, but her first impressions were of the strong, sensuous mouth that was twisted into a wry grin of amusement at her predicament. Then she looked at the rest of his face, the high-bridged, once-broken nose, the broad, tanned forehead and crown of light brown, wavy hair. She was immediately and uncomfortably conscious of her own grimy crumpled appearance, especially when it compared to his well-cut Harris tweed jacket and knife-edged trousers. There was nothing soft about this man, nor anything subtle, either.

His eyes prowled along Riley's body, pausing provocatively at the soft swell of her breasts, the narrowness of her tiny waist. Then they returned to meet her own eyes with a directness that was decidedly refreshing after the smarmy attitude of the banker.

Refreshing ... and infuriating! What he said next only added to that.

'I don't even want to move the car just now. But I would like to get into the back and your truck is rather blocking the back door.'

Riley threw a glance in the direction indicated, drew a quick, angry breath, then returned to meet his eyes with a scornful sneer.

'Are you really that helpless?' she snarled. 'Or was it just easier to hassle me than to climb over the back seat and get whatever the hell you wanted?'

'What? And miss finding out what could combine those very elegant legs with that bullock-driver's vocabulary?'

'Well, I hope you're satisfied,' she retorted, yanking her wrist free from his grasp. Without waiting for his reply, she knelt down to slide back beneath the truck.

'Very much so,' was the reply, in a smug, self-satisfied voice that sent lightning bolts of anger surging through her. 'It was well worth making my bank manager wait.'

She couldn't help the retort; it shot past her lips like a runaway bulldozer.

'Well, if he's anything like mine, that's all the satisfaction you'll get today, so have another look and welcome to it,' she snarled as she slid back under the truck, away from those pervasive eyes.

'So that's it,' came the calm reply, and she glanced round to see that he had made no move at all to depart. 'You're heaping all this abuse on me and your poor old truck just because you've had problems at the bank. If you were looking to borrow money to set up as a mechanic, I'm hardly surprised he knocked you back; the cleaning bills would eat up your profits just as a snack.'

Riley's hasty blow with the largest spanner rang from the concrete an inch from his toe, but she got at least some measure of satisfaction in seeing his foot jerk backwards.

Satisfaction—but shortlived!

Her growl of pleasure changed to a squeal of dismay when fingers of steel tightened round her ankle and she was plucked from beneath the truck, the spanner waving wildly in one hand but her skirt up round her waist and both legs waving even more wildly.

'There may be some excuse for common language, but common assault is something else again,' he said calmly, still holding one ankle in the air while he deftly avoided both the frantic and the vicious swipes from the spanner.

'Damn you! Let me go!'

'Not until I can be sure you're not likely to brain me with that thing!' And his eyes spread his grin into frank, undisguised laughter.

'Brain you? I'll un-man you!' she threatened, but the attempt was as futile as the words and did nothing but leave her increasingly aware of his touch on her ankle and his visual caress of her body.

'Temper, temper,' he said, but the voice was anything but soothing to her already white-hot anger. How dared he? On top of the patronising innuendo she had already endured that morning, this man's idle caress was too much!

'I'll "temper" you!' she cried, and swung frantically in yet another attempt to connect with the spanner. It hit the concrete with a resounding clang, then slipped from her fingers as he reached down to claim both her wrists and haul her upright.

'Much as I was enjoying the view, I must admit this isn't quite the time or the place,' he grinned.

Riley's response would have blistered the hardiest of old-time bullock-drivers, but it only served to provoke a wider grin from this infuriating man.

'Enough, I said.' His tone was cautionary, his grip on her wrists becoming painful.

'I'll give you enough!' she replied, so angry now that she hardly knew what she was saying. She looked around desperately, hoping there might be somebody in sight to whom she could appeal for help.

A futile hope.

She opted for the next best possibility, and aimed a knee at the annoying stranger's most vulnerable target.

'Now *that* was downright nasty,' he said, casually

turning her so the attack merely grazed his muscular thigh. And then he was holding her firmly by the shoulders and shaking her.

'Right,' he said grimly, when her world had steadied a moment later. 'Now maybe you'll take a moment to listen, instead of launching some new attack before I've a chance to say anything. But it's up to you—do you listen or do I have to shake some sense into you?'

Riley gritted her teeth in silence, seeking to destroy him with her eyes, with the intensity of her anger. She focused that rage upon him, glaring into those hazel depths as she sought the most direct route to burn out his soul.

Their eyes met, locked, and for what seemed like days they stayed that way. Until he spoke.

'That's better, I suppose.' His grin was smugly victorious. 'Unless of course you're really the witch you're trying to be. And if you were that good at it, you'd have been able to fix the truck without getting your face all smudged, so I guess I don't have too much to worry about on that score.'

'Get stuf . . .'

'*No*!' He used the tone one might reserve for a boisterous puppy, and Riley shut up, half expecting him next to say, 'Sit!' in exactly the same tone—and expect obedience.

'Much better,' he finally said, voice slightly softer after an eternity in which their eyes locked in a battle of wills that Riley was gradually realising she couldn't win. 'Now, instead of indulging in this rather silly brawl, what do you say to a truce so that I can talk to you without worrying about getting my head knocked off?'

'All right,' she sighed, most of her energy drained in any event. But when he released her, she immediately stepped back to give herself room, breathing space.

The touch of his fingers remained like handcuffs on

her wrists, a curious mixture of warmth and chill. Like the effect his steady, almost haughty appraisal had upon her. Riley could feel that appraisal penetrating far beneath the surface, slicing past her smudged face and filthy hands—and equally past the remains of her once lovely business outfit.

'Right,' he finally said. And smiled at her, this time almost engagingly. 'Now that we've got that settled, how about looking at ways I might be of some actual assistance? My first suggestion being that I arrange for a proper mechanic, since neither of us is really dressed for this type of work today.'

'Well, it's a bit late on my part!' she retorted, glaring first at him and then at her grimy hands and ruined blouse. 'And if I could have paid a mechanic, I'd have had one here already.'

'Do you really have the faintest idea what you're doing under there?' he asked, ignoring her still-angry attitude.

'Of course I know what I'm doing!' she cried, the reply only just short of a scream. 'I'd already have it done if some people didn't insist on interrupting!'

'You didn't seem to be doing all that well when I got here,' he replied calmly. 'Or was all that cursing just for effect?'

'All part of the service,' Riley said in a deep-frozen voice, not remotely inclined to reveal how embarrassed she was at the ease with which this haughty stranger seemed to bring out the worst in her. 'So, thanks for the offer—no, I don't need help, but if you *insist* on being helpful the nicest thing you could do is just ... go ... away!'

'Rather than slide under there and loosen or tighten whatever it is that seems to be beyond your ability?' There could have been a sneer in his voice, a subtle hint of chauvinism. She wasn't sure.

'What—so we can both get filthy? No, thank you!
Besides, I can manage quite easily; it's just a matter of
leverage, that's all.'

'Yes, I should think so,' he mused, then added,
'leverage that must be a bit tricky to combine with
proper modesty.' And the eyes that strayed to her
thoroughly crumpled skirt finished that comment.

'I . . . well . . .'

She couldn't really argue with that, despite the fact
that before his arrival she hadn't given modesty much
thought. Now, however, she found the thought of
sprawling under the truck with her skirt up around her
hips distinctly off-putting.

Suddenly he grinned, and it was a genuine, warm
grin, the smile of a co-conspirator. More importantly, it
somehow showed that he was understanding her
predicament and was no longer going to rub her nose in
it.

'I suppose if I offered to pay for the mechanic you'd
get all stuffy and offended,' he mused, speaking as much
to himself as to Riley and giving her no chance to reply
before he continued, 'so the next best thing is to provide
you with a bit of cover while you get on with the job,
eh?'

And before she could do more than gasp with
surprise, he had taken her hand and was guiding her
into a position where she could easily slide back under
the truck. Even as she hauled herself into the contorted
position she required to free that final, stubborn bolt,
she felt his fingers gently pull down the hem of her skirt
into the most modest position possible. Under the
circumstances!

When she looked, it was to see only the back of him as
he squatted in order to conceal her from any passing
eyes. The work took only a moment, then, and when she
slid from beneath the truck for the final time, the

wreckage of the tailshaft in one begrimed fist, he was there to help her to her feet and steady her as she flung the heavy truck part into the tray.

'That was quick,' he grinned, somehow managing to make the comment into a compliment beyond its spoken value.

Riley grinned in return. 'It's just a bit easier to work when you don't have to worry about being had up for indecent exposure! Thank you very much for that.'

'My pleasure. Now what do you say to a cup of coffee, or better yet a drink? I think you've earned a spot of celebration.'

'Looking like this?' She glanced at her grease-stained hands and the smears that guaranteed the ruination of her blouse, then twisted her lips in a grimace of distaste. 'Thanks, but no, thanks. It's home and a hot bath for me—after I've installed the new tailshaft that's waiting. And speaking of waiting, didn't you say you were already late for an appointment with your bank manager?'

'He can wait.'

There was an assured confidence to the statement, a blatant arrogance. Clearly this tall, undeniably attractive stranger had no qualms about handling *his* bank manager.

Just your luck, Riley thought, suddenly feeling less than confident herself now that the crisis was over and she could only face custom tailoring from the disadvantage of her own grubby appearance. It was bad enough to have made such a spectacle of herself, without now having to endure his continued scrutiny when she looked so disreputable. He read her thoughts.

'Stop being so defensive. I'm sure you brush up quite acceptably.'

The comment, accompanied by a wicked grin at her immediate flush of surprise, instantly rekindled the very defensiveness he was so quick to laugh at.

'It isn't funny,' Riley snapped, then stifled a gasp of
alarm as he placed one strong hand at the back of her
neck and easily shifted her round so that she was forced
to meet her own gaze in the side-mirror of the utility.

'Isn't it?' he asked. His laugh was more than just
mildly wicked—it was sheer devilment.

'No, damn it! It isn't!' But her anger was directed as
much at herself as at her captor. The grease-smudged
face that grimaced back at her only served to heighten
her dismay and embarrassment.

Riley stamped her foot, narrowly missing his instep
with one high heel, and although she hadn't meant it as
a renewed assault, there was tremendous satisfaction in
his immediate release of her as he stepped away.

'Oh, no. Not that approach again!' he said grimly.
And the chuckle in that deep, vibrant voice was
suddenly hard-edged, wary. 'You save your aggression
for the bankers, lady, or this is the last time I ever help
you fix this monstrosity of a machine.'

'Well, I should certainly hope so,' she snarled. It was
enough that he had first manhandled her, then added
insult to injury by helping her. But to malign her poor
old truck was the final straw! She launched herself into
the driver's seat of the truck and slammed the door after
her, fingers already seeking the ignition key.

Her exit, however, was far from the high-handed,
independent gesture she might have wished for. First
she had to put the vehicle into four-wheel-drive, so that
the front-wheel-drive could move it. Then she had to
ease away gently to avoid any roll-back that would have
seen her trailer-hitch smashing her arrogant saviour's
tail lights.

He stood calmly, hands on hips, and watched the
performance with a slight downcurve of those generous,
sensuous lips. And there was no satisfaction at all in

having to drive away up the ramp, knowing she must eventually turn round and descend past him.

Riley delayed that manoeuvre as long as she could by driving right to the open-air top level before turning the truck around. She then spent a moment scrubbing at her grimy fingers with a rag, but finally had no delaying tactic left, short of parking and taking the elevator down to where she could visit the washrooms for a decent scrub-up. He was still standing there when she drove past. Standing, eyes laughing at her, he gave a magnanimous bow, like a bullfighter waving to the bull.

CHAPTER TWO

JULIUS GUNN'S voice, despite more than thirty years in Australia, still held strong traces of his Germanic origins, especially on the telephone.

'I have maybe some work for you. Tomorrow in the morning at seven we will go to look at a forest,' he said, not bothering to inform Riley who was speaking, much less to enquire if his plans might be convenient to her.

It wasn't really rudeness, just his way. And even if it *had* been rude, she would gleefully have ignored the rudeness in the face of possible work.

Work! Or at least the chance of work, which put her a thousand per cent ahead of where she'd been that morning. Or even at noon, when she'd been slowly manouevring the labouring truck homeward.

Now, at least, she was cleaner, having only just emerged from the long, soaking bath she had promised the infuriating stranger of the car park. Equally important, the truck was fixed and going well.

'What kind of work? What's it all about?' she asked breathlessly, knowing Julius was capable of hanging up without so much as goodbye.

'Maybe something; maybe nothing. We must first go and see,' he replied cryptically. Then, to Riley's great surprise, he sighed deeply and continued.

'Very much this depends on you. If where we go is the place I'm thinking, the place that I remember, we could have good logging for one year, maybe two.'

'But—but how can it depend on me?' she asked, now totally confused.

'In the morning, as we go, I will explain.' And before

she could even think to ask more, he *had* hung up.

The frustration of it was almost more than Riley could bear. For one fleeting instant, she even considered phoning Bill to see if he could tell her. As heir-apparent to the family sawmilling business, he would surely know.

Then common sense took hold.

She could ask Bill, and if he knew, he would surely tell her. But the price, Riley knew only too well, would be a renewed surge in his campaign to push her into marriage. Ever since the funeral, Bill had been subtly working up to the subject, held at bay only by her fierce refusal even to discuss the possibility.

No, she could not deliberately put herself in his debt. It was bad enough that she was compelled to accept whatever work Julius might throw her way, though at least the old man, whatever his chauvinism, accepted Riley's abilities without question—as well he should, she thought.

But Julius' enigmatic approach to things didn't help. As she prepared for bed, Riley couldn't avoid wondering why she, personally, should have such importance in the scheme of things tomorrow.

She pondered the matter into restless sleep, but was no closer to knowing when she waited in the frosty stillness of morning, her breath steaming into the darkness as she watched for the vehicle lights that would herald Julius' arrival. She wore faded jeans and a work-shirt, steel-toed Blundstone work-boots and a warm, down-filled vest to cut the chill. Her hard hat and axe rested on the stoop.

Julius was far from communicative during the early minutes of their journey, but once they'd driven south to reach the Arthur Highway, he seemed to relax slightly.

'I need you for this because I must have a logging

contractor who is also a conservationist,' he blurted without preamble.

Riley raised one dark eyebrow, but said nothing, her face revealing little of the immediate turmoil that simple statement caused inside her. The way he had spat out that final word, as if it were something in his mouth that tasted foul, was sufficient warning to put her immediately on guard.

Julius seemed to accept her silence; he drove for several kilometres before continuing, and when he did go on, it was in an almost apologetic tone.

'Yesterday I went to the bank in Hobart,' he began. 'My bank manager knows of the problems we have finding private sawlogs, and he arranged this meeting with another of his customers, a man named Devereux.'

Julius looked at Riley, who merely shrugged. The name meant nothing to her. What did mean something was the knowledge that Julius had the same banker as she did.

For a moment her mind went blank; red rage blotted out every other thought as she considered how the annoying little man had refused her every request, while obviously considering Julius Gunn's problems from quite a different viewpoint.

'This man, Devereux, he was very late for the meeting, but it seems he has about a thousand acres of forest that he has only recently inherited, and if it *is* the parcel I think it is—well, I didn't mind waiting,' Julius went on. 'It's prime forest. I tried to make an arrangement with the woman who owned it—I think it was his aunt, or something—but she didn't want any logging on it at all.'

'And this—Devereux? He does?'

Julius shrugged. 'He is at least willing to discuss it, which is more than the woman would do. She

threatened to run me off with a shotgun just for
mentioning it.'

Riley sat in silence for some time. Then, 'But he at
least talked to you about it yesterday. I still don't see
where I fit in.'

Julius' grin was shark-like.

'He, too, is a conservationist, but at least, I think, a
reasonable one. We will see.'

'That doesn't answer my question.'

'It should. What he wants is somebody to log it very
selectively, very tidily. He has plans, I think, to develop
the area as a private forest on a long-term basis, maybe
partly in plantation.'

'And you think I'll at least be able to talk his
language,' Riley muttered, half to Julius and half to
herself in a tone that flattered neither.

This is all I need, she thought. A land-owner who's
crazy about conservation, and who probably expects
you can put a bulldozer through the bush as neatly as
you put a rotary hoe through a cultivated garden patch.

Riley was herself a conservationist, but she had no
time or patience for the 'ratbag' element that had
emerged throughout the conservation movement to
preach against all forms of development without
displaying one iota of real knowledge or common sense.
Having grown up with the bitterly divisive Franklin
Dam controversy, she was now totally and cynically
sceptical of rabid conservationists—and all politicians!
The more so now that the attention of both seemed fated
to focus upon the state's forest industries.

She had been appalled at how quickly the Franklin
issue had degenerated into a political dog-fight that
removed any chance of a rational settlement, and she
was smart enough to realise that a focus on the forest
industries would result in the same situation.

'*Is* that why you've brought me along—so that if he

turns out to be a radical conservationist you'll have somebody to try and bring him into line?'

Not that it would do much good if that were the case, Riley thought. Although perhaps better she than most of Julius Gunn's logging contractors. Most were so bitter at the unreasoning and unreasonable arguments of the vocal conservation minority that they'd sooner fight then try to make rational conversation with anyone who displayed obvious *greenie* attitudes.

'If he were a radical conservationist, we would not be going to look at his forest,' Julius replied calmly. 'I am thinking he is a reasonable man who wants only to do the best thing for the future development of his land. If this is true, I have not the knowledge to advise him properly. But you do.'

Riley was stunned into silence by that remark.

'There are plenty of people better suited to it than I am,' she said finally. 'Surely he would have sought advice from the private forestry division, just for a start.'

Julius shrugged. 'Perhaps he has. I know that he has worked out some form of management plan, and that he feels there are a good number of sawlogs that should be harvested before they become over-mature.'

He then dropped the information that Devereux's aunt had held the property for something like sixty years, and at no time during that period had any logging whatsoever been allowed on it. 'I had a quick look at some of the country about ten years ago, and it was very good timber then.'

It should have satisfied Riley, but instead she grew more and more apprehensive as their drive took them closer to the property in question. She had her own definite ideas on forest management, and they didn't always totally coincide with those promulgated by other facets of the forest industry.

So how would they be accepted by a man who had inherited a property where logging had been banned for longer than she had been alive?

Their journey took them along the Arthur Highway only briefly, then Julius turned north-eastward, along a gravel road through Wattle Hill. Riley knew if they continued long enough they'd pass Nugent and eventually return to the Tasman Highway just east of Buckland.

But they turned north-west before Nugent, and began working their way upward towards the slopes of Nelson's Tier and Linger Longer Hill.

Riley's apprehension grew, enough so that she began to worry about herself. It was as if some wicked spirit had singled her out for special, mischievous treatment.

But why? The name Devereux meant nothing to her. And she had never, to her memory, been on this road before, or even anywhere near.

The small, tidy white cottage that hove into view when they turned a sharp bend in the track was in no way familiar. But the figure that stepped on to the porch as they approached was, only she couldn't figure out why—until he stepped out into the revealing sunlight.

The man from the car park!

Riley gave a small gasp of astonishment, then slid down in her seat, deliberately ignoring the questioning glance Julius shot her.

Her eyes peeped over the dashboard of the truck, but even as her mind claimed she must be imagining things, she knew instinctively what she would see. That same tall, rangy figure, the shock of untidy, light brown hair, and the laughing hazel eyes warm with welcome as he approached the driver's side and greeted Julius.

Then he looked past the older man, and his eyes flickered through a range of expressions before settling on suspicion as he raised one dark eyebrow in a gesture that could only indicate recognition.

'I thought you were bringing your logging contractor?' he asked, glance shooting from Riley to Julius and back again.

The unsaid 'not your girl-friend' was too obvious to ignore, and Riley felt her temper curdling up in her throat. Her eyes flashed fire as she struggled to hold her temper long enough to answer, but Julius spoke first.

'I have done so,' he replied quietly, with nothing in voice or attitude indicating that he might have caught the implied slur Riley was certain she'd picked up.

'Riley Jones—Freyn Devereux.'

Neither party replied to the introduction immediately. Riley was too busy enjoying the look of astonishment that flickered across Devereux's face, followed by a frown that immediately put her on guard.

'Miss Jones,' he nodded then, and she could only nod in reply, not quite trusting herself to speak.

Freyn Devereux! A rather unusual name, she thought, and only fitting to the man who bore it. Despite the drastic change in attire, from sophisticated city gear to the casual flannel shirt and soft corduroy trousers he now wore, there was no disguising the slim, muscular body or the cat-like movements.

Or the quickness of decision.

'Slide over, Miss Jones,' he said curtly, striding round the front of the truck to wrench open her door and plunk himself in beside her.

Riley had no choice, and was crushed between the two men as Freyn gave Julius directions.

Once past the cottage, the track became progressively rougher, and Riley found herself being thrown violently from side to side as the vehicle lurched its way up into the forest. The roughness, however, was nothing compared to the feeling of Freyn Devereux's arm tucked protectively around her shoulders, and the way his grip served to steady her through the worst sections. He was forced to lean across in front of her as he issued directions, and she was increasingly aware of the strength of him, of the warmth of his thigh against hers, the way his grip pulled her shoulder against the firmness of his chest. Despite the casual clothing, he was freshly shaven, and the tangy freshness of his after-shave seemed to hover like an aura around both of them. It was a pleasant, slightly musky scent, subtle and yet positive. Certainly an improvement over the peat-bog-and-heather cologne the banker favoured!

But Devereux's forest was somewhat less impressive. As Riley had expected, it was badly overcrowded and thick with over-mature timber that was of no real economic value.

They spent the next hour driving along the myriad tracks that traversed the property, gaining a general over-view of what timber might be available and what the access situation might be. Then came the real evaluation, and this had to be done on foot.

Freyn Devereux stepped lithely down from the vehicle, then turned and offered his hand to Riley, who was already emerging behind him. She paused, half in and half out of the truck, then realised she had little choice in the matter, and accepted his courtesy.

Perhaps it was only her imagination that he held her fingers just a bit longer than necessary, but there was no doubting the intensity of his glance, the way his eyes swept across her slender figure from hard hat to steel-toed boots.

Riley forced herself to meet his eyes, even as she found the right words to thank him for helping her down. But she found it impossible to read anything in their hazel depths except perhaps a mild curiosity.

'I liked your mechanic's outfit better,' he said then, in a voice so low she barely heard. Laughter danced in his eyes at her startled expression.

'It would hardly be appropriate out here,' she finally managed to reply, then quickly turned away and picked up her axe from the tray of the truck.

'I'll just have a wander up along that ridge there,' she said to Julius, pointing in the direction she intended to go. 'There looked to be some pretty fair stringy barks and maybe a blue gum or two.'

Julius pointed first to himself and then in the opposite direction to indicate his intentions. They needed little conversation; both knew their jobs and what they must look for in the way of suitable timber.

Riley struck off uphill, moving straight into the thick underbrush with the confidence born of long experience. Behind her—and why did it come as no surprise?—she could hear Freyn Devereux following.

She took some inexplicable satisfaction in finding that he moved through the bush almost as surely as she herself. But there was less satisfaction in the fact that she could actually *feel* his eyes on her, and that her jeans were too well-worn, too well-fitting.

'You really needn't have come,' she commented over her shoulder.

'What, and risk you getting lost or something? Besides, I'm rather intrigued by all this. You might be a little less antagonistic and try telling me what it is that you're looking for.'

There was a slender hint of laughter in his voice, almost an admission that he had only come because he knew it would grate on her nerves.

'I'm looking for trees that will make sawlogs,' she replied grudgingly, wondering immediately why she should be feeling so defensive, so vulnerable.

'And I gather you think I'm in your way?'

'Of course not. It's just that I'm—well—I suppose I'm a bit defensive after that performance yesterday. And a bit surprised at finding you here today.'

'No more surprised than I was,' he replied, and she could hear the chuckle in his voice, the almost teasing sound that might come from someone who had shared a secret. It was decidedly disconcerting.

'So how do you judge a sawlog?' he asked, after Riley had walked on without further comment, her mind only half on the job at hand.

'Oh, it isn't that difficult. Size, girth, that sort of thing,' she replied vaguely, continuing to walk, her eyes now searching through the larger timber, assessing, evaluating.

'So how about this one?'

Damn, she thought. He was determined to force her into conversation whether she liked it or not.

'Too crooked,' she replied automatically, and would have continued walking.

'Hang on!'

She had no choice. Fingers like steel caught at her shoulder, halting her in her tracks—but not harshly; it was a surprisingly gentle, if firm, restraint.

'How can you possibly call that tree crooked?' he asked directly. 'It's as straight as a die!'

Riley fought back the astonishing sense of panic his grip had caused, and when she replied it was in a voice deliberately light and cheerful. 'The trunk's straight up and down, but the grain is so twisted it would never make a sawlog. Just look at the bark and you'll see what I mean. Even for category two, the requirement is no less than one-in-eight.'

Freyn stepped back, releasing her and shifting his position to give himself a better look at the tall blue gum. He regarded the tree soberly for some moments, then turned back to Riley.

'Okay, I think I see what you mean,' he said. 'So what about this one over here?'

Riley walked over to the tree he indicated, her eye expertly running a judgment of height and girth. She looked back at Freyn, who stood calmly, awaiting her judgment.

'It looks all right,' she admitted, then fetched the trunk a hefty thump with the back of her axe. The dullness of the sound told its own story. 'No good,' she said. 'It's got the woodmen in it.'

'Which means?'

'White-ants. Termites. The centre will be eaten out, or rotten. No good for lumber.'

He looked unconvinced.

'And you can tell that just by the sound?'

'Not infallibly, but usually, yes.' She whacked the offending tree again, then walked to one only a few feet away and gave it the same treatment.

'Hear the difference in the sound?'

His response was accompanied by a surprisingly warm grin, considering. 'No, but I'll take your word for it. I suppose I'll have to, or you'll be thumping *me* to see if I'm rotten inside!'

'I don't need an axe for that!' Riley quipped. Let him take that remark any way he wished to, she thought. This Freyn Devereux was far too sure of himself for her taste.

Yet when she looked at him, half expecting some clever response, she found only a curious softness in his glance. And he didn't reply at all.

They moved on then, walking side by side in the more open going, and when Riley struck off down the other side of the ridge, he waited for her at the crest, seemingly deep in thoughts of his own.

More than an hour passed in that fashion, with Freyn moving slowly up the crest of the ridge while Riley quartered back and forth, thumping a tree here and there with the axe, her mind busily compiling an overall picture of the forest as she wandered.

Julius was waiting when they returned to the truck, and Riley could tell from his expression that he, too, had been impressed by the quantity and quality of available sawlogs.

'Let's go back to the house for coffee, presuming you've seen enough,' Devereux suggested, and it was an idea gladly taken up.

The tiny cottage, Riley imagined, was just as it had been when Devereux's aunt had lived there. Immaculate, clearly designed for the over-tidy needs of a person living alone and happy with that life-style, it was like a doll's house with the two large masculine figures in it. A well-arranged kitchen took up the sunny side of the house, and the lounge room was beautifully furnished in old-style leather. Comfortable furniture, lived-in furniture. It all shouted out how much the old lady had loved her home, her property. What it didn't say was how her misguided ideas had allowed the forest to deteriorate— at least from a commercial point of view. It was something Freyn Devereux would have to be told, but Riley didn't relish being the one to tell him.

And yet she would have to; he would insist on it.

Freyn made the coffee, moving about the small kitchen with the ease of long familiarity. Riley wondered how much time he must have spent here, and found herself also wondering how close he had been to the aunt she had never met. The forest aside, she felt an overwhelming empathy with Freyn's aunt. Despite having never met her, Riley could see from the house, the tidy garden, the loving care that had been expended on the property, that she might very well have liked the woman who had made it her domain for so long.

There was no immediate rush to discuss the business of the day. Freyn and Julius spent some time talking about general subjects, sounding each other out in the subtle—or supposedly subtle—way that men have. Riley stayed quiet and just listened, finding their gentle verbal fencing transparent as glass and wondering if they, too, realised just how transparent it all was.

Eventually talk turned to the forest, and immediately she was all ears, because this was her own speciality, not to mention the topic on which would depend her immediate future!

'Sawlogs, there are plenty,' Julius said. 'Not always so easy to get, however, because much of the country is very steep. Still, that is Riley's problem.'

'How much of a problem?'

Riley took her time answering. She knew that there were elements to the ultimate decision that put her in something of a position of power, but her assessment of Freyn Devereux made her instinctively cautious.

'That will depend a lot on the weather,' she finally said. 'If it stays dry, things would go fairly easy. But if it rains a lot this winter . . .'

'You will need the bulldozer anyway.' That was Julius with his pragmatic approach.

'Yes,' she agreed. 'There is a lot of good timber in areas too steep for the skidder.'

'Mr Devereux has to me mentioned the situation of how much mess will be made.'

Riley took a deep breath, unsure whether Julius' candour was a good thing or not. No logging operation, to untrained eyes, is less than messy, but she had hoped to stave off this aspect of the discussion. Now, feeling Freyn's eyes on her, she was compelled to reply.

'If this is something that concerns Mr Devereux, then we'd best talk about it now,' she agreed, knowing that Julius felt he was in a position to deal, but still unsure exactly what her own part in the scheme of things would be.

'It does concern me,' Freyn said without preamble.

'As Mr Gunn knows, and I suppose he's told you, Miss Jones, my aunt was—well, almost fanatical about not allowing logging on this property.'

'Which is a pity, in many ways,' Riley interrupted, 'because her fanaticism has caused a lot of problems for the very forest she was trying to protect.'

Julius, at this point, shot her a venomous look that told her to desist, but at Freyn's inquisitive glance, she felt compelled to continue.

'Just look at it,' she said. 'There's so much over-mature, practically useless timber about that there's no room for the good young growth. The best of the sawlogs should have beem taken out of here ten years ago. And there's so much rubbish about on the ground that when you do get a fire, it will cause untold damage.'

'You don't sound impressed.'

And neither did Freyn Devereux. Riley caught the glint of steel in his voice, the slight undertone that warned her to caution.

But it was too late. 'No, I'm not impressed,' she heard herself saying, and half her mind screamed at her to shut up before she blew the entire situation.

'Look, Mr Devereux, I'm sure your aunt meant the very best by what she was doing. But she—well, she didn't have the expertise, and if she was following somebody else's advice I have to say it wasn't the best advice. This forest is a mess.

'Oh, there are some excellent sawlogs. Enough, I suppose, to keep me busy for six months or a year or maybe more. But in the long term, the forest has suffered because of the vast number of over-mature trees that have inhibited growth of younger, better trees, and because, in the areas where young timber has started to come on, it hasn't been thinned, so it's had no room to grow.'

'And yet you do agree there is a quantity of good

sawlogs?' He didn't wait for an answer. 'Accepting, of course, that sawlogs are all you're interested in?'

'I am interested in sawlogs, yes,' Riley replied in a chill voice, unable to put away the feeling that he was leading her now, drawing her into saying something that she oughtn't. Julius' expression seemed to confirm that; the old sawmiller was fairly livid, his face red and his eyes bulging with suppressed anger.

'But that isn't what you asked about,' she continued with force. 'You asked about the forest as a whole, and that's what I'm talking about. Not this year's harvest, or next year's, but the future of your forest as a renewable resource, something for your children and your grandchildren to have.'

'You do plan ahead.'

And his tone caused her to look at him, seeking some clue in those deep hazel eyes to tell her where he was trying to lead this discussion. She couldn't tell. Freyn Devereux's eyes were like mirrors, revealing nothing of what he felt, what he thought.

'I suppose next you'll be telling me the best thing is to bulldoze the whole thing down and start afresh, with a pine plantation, for instance?'

'On the basis of today's very sparse tour of the forest, I'd not be prepared to say any such thing,' Riley replied heatedly. 'All I can talk about is what I saw, and that's what I've done. Only a damned fool would advise clear-felling for a pine plantation on the limited information I've gathered today.'

At this point Julius interjected, clearly concerned that there might be a slanging match if he didn't.

'Our business is sawlogs, not pine trees,' he proclaimed sternly. 'Sawlogs I need, and sawlogs you have. But if you wish to discuss overall forest management with Riley, I must ask for it to be some other time. I have other appointments today and must leave soon.'

Freyn accepted the comments without apparent rancour. He turned to Riley without bothering to answer Julius, and asked, 'And what about you, Miss Jones? Do you also have other appointments?'

Did she? Riley had to look to Julius for the answer, unsure if even *his* appointments were genuine, or if he was simply trying to get her out of the place because he could sense the growing discord between herself and Freyn Devereux.

I—I must of course depend on Julius for transportation,' she said evasively, having received no help whatsoever from the sawmill owner.

It sounded exactly the lame excuse that it was, but Freyn seemed to ignore the nuances.

'Presuming you're also based at Orielton, that's no worry at all,' he said. 'I have to return to the city later today, so it's no trouble to drop you off.'

And then, as if he could read Riley's indecisiveness and—quite correctly—the reasons for it, he added the unarguable clincher.

'Please,' he said. 'I don't feel it would be right for me to make any decision on the sawlogs without as much overall information as I can find, and you seem reasonably qualified to provide some of that.'

'She is very well qualified. She was nearly at the top of her class in forestry when she was forced to drop out of university,' Julius interposed, and Riley stifled a gasp of surprise at the comment. How had Julius known that? She looked at the old sawmiller apprehensively, assessing his role as family friend with new eyes.

Then Freyn replied by saying, 'Well, I knew she wasn't a motor mechanic!' and Riley's attention spun back again to the younger man. She saw, as she might have expected, a fire of inner laughter in those hazel eyes, but Julius, to her great relief, didn't understand the joke.

'She is better than most qualified mechanics when it comes to logging equipment,' he declared stoutly, quite astonishing Riley with the firmness of his defence.

'And if we can come to some arrangement regarding the sawlogs on this property, I presume she would be the logging contractor of your choice?' Freyn asked.

A rather stupid question, Riley thought. Julius had brought her along specifically with that in mind, and had already made that clear.

'Unless you have some specific objection,' the old man replied, not meeting Riley's eyes as he prepared to sell her out, perhaps.

'And if I did?' Freyn didn't so much as glance at Riley when he asked the question. She might not have been there.

Julius, ever the pragmatist, merely shrugged, at first.

'I have other contractors; the choice is for you to make,' he said finally. 'But for what you want, and the way you wish to have the work done, she is the best I can offer.'

Riley sat in stunned silence, confused by the ludicrous mixture of recommendation and potential rejection. She was mightily tempted to throw something hard and pointed at Julius, but with her future so clearly in the balance she didn't dare.

Then she caught a sideways glance from Freyn Devereux and noticed the laughter lurking there. Damn him! He was deliberately fomenting this discussion, and all the time he was doing it he knew Riley was being tormented.

She caught her breath, biting her tongue to keep down the outburst that threatened to erupt in a stream of vitriolic comment that would put the infuriating Mr Devereux in his place. Only she dared not speak, because to speak would be to shout, rage, scream out her defiance of his beastly advantage-taking.

And then, astonishingly, it wasn't necessary.

'Certainly she would be my choice also,' Freyn said. 'I think her overall advice might be invaluable.'

Riley was still trying to figure out the ambiguity of his attitude as Freyn escorted Julius back to his truck, returning a moment later to pour fresh coffee for the two of them. He brought the coffee to the table, placed hers carefully in front of her, then sprawled comfortably in the chair across from her.

'You can stop worrying now; I've told Gunn I'll accept his royalty offer,' Freyn said without preamble. 'Does that give you enough leverage to go and spit in your banker's eye?'

Riley looked up in some surprise. How could he do it? The first thought in her mind after his disclosure, and he'd picked it up straight away!

'I'd like to,' she admitted. 'But all this will do is give me some breathing space on the repayment situation. Judging from his reaction yesterday, I can't imagine him agreeing to a re-finance scheme just because I've finally got a bit of work in hand.'

'So why not change bankers? Yours, in particular, couldn't be of much use to somebody in your business. He doesn't know a thing about it.'

'H . . . how . . .?'

He grinned, eyes alight with laughter at her surprise.

'Easy enough—I saw the chequebook on your truck seat yesterday, which told me the bank, and having you turn up today with Julius Gunn, who, you might remember, was introduced to me by our mutual bank manager—well, it wasn't all that tricky to make the connections!'

'But I suppose you're terrifically impressed with yourself for doing it,' Riley countered, shrinking back into her chair with the caution of a cornered animal. She did not like this! Freyn Devereux had involved himself

far too much in her affairs during the twenty-four hours
since they'd first met, and it left her with few defences.
She glared at him over her coffee cup, feeling distinctly
at a disadvantage.

'I suppose your next move is to offer to intervene with
the bank manager for me—at a price!' she suggested,
voice harsh with derision.

'With him? Not a chance! Like I said, he's of little use
to you at the best of times.'

Freyn either hadn't noticed or chose to ignore the
scorn in Riley's question. He appeared to have taken it
seriously, and was replying in that vein.

'But, if you are thinking of changing banks, I know a
banker whose knowledge of primary industries might
make him at least a possible ally,' he continued.
'Provided your proposal makes some economic sense,
that is.'

'I thought it did. Now I'm not so sure,' replied Riley,
still cautious, but curious at the same time. Why should
this man want to help her? Especially when he was
operating from such a position of power.

She paused, and when Freyn made no move to speak,
she eventually blurted out her concerns.

'I don't understand why you'd want to be involved at
all,' she said. 'You only met me yesterday, after all, and
not under the most promising circumstances, either. I
just don't see what's in it for you.'

'I'm after your body, of course!'

But he was lying, or at least mostly lying. Everything
about him, eyes, mouth, total expression, told her that.
Besides, she didn't imagine this man would need that
kind of persuasion to get most girls into his bed.

'I do wish you'd either be serious or frivolous, and not
both at the same time,' sighed Riley with a frown. 'I find
it very difficult to make any sense out of you this way.'

His laugh was almost, but not quite, infectious.

'All right, serious,' he said. 'Yes, there is a price, but not anything I'd expect you to have problems with. The truth is that I do need advice about what to do with this damned forest, and I need professional advice based, as you said earlier, on long term.'

'Which makes me the worst person to ask,' Riley interrupted. 'I'm just a bit biased, don't you see? After all, my best advantage is served by getting out as many sawlogs as possible, as quickly as possible, and with as little effort as I can manage!'

'That's a rather short-term viewpoint, and a pretty stupid one at that,' Freyn declared. 'Especially following our earlier discussions. Try remembering how clearly it was established that you, pretty as you are, can hardly be considered irreplaceable. Cross me, and Julius Gunn would have you going down the road with your tail between your legs in thirty seconds flat!'

'Well, he might not have to wait for the chance,' Riley retorted. 'I don't see how you can expect me to do my job properly if you're going to be holding that over my head! I might as well pack it in right now; it would save me the trouble of bringing in my equipment!'

'You'd be wiser to take the trouble to just hang on to your temper,' was the response. 'I'm not trying to hold anything over your head. I'm just saying that what I want from you is more than just somebody to cut down trees and whatever else logging contractors do. I want some proper, long-term planning before you even start, and since I realise you can't make money from Gunn by delaying your logging operation, I'm prepared to make it worth your while myself. Surely there's nothing wrong in that?'

'Even the best of dogs can't serve two masters,' Riley replied almost without thinking.

'Hardly relevant, since you're certainly not a dog,' he answered. 'Or at least not a male dog; I'll withhold judgment on the obvious option!'

'Oh!'

But that was all she could say. The implication of his remark was like a slap in the face.

"'*Oh*?" Surely you can do better than that?'

'I shan't bother,' she said, struggling to hold any semblance of composure. She looked across the table into those incredible hazel eyes and felt as if the room was closing in around her, forcing her closer and closer to Freyn Devereux. It was unnerving, unsettling, yet somehow there was a lure of pleasure.

Then logic returned, and she set down the coffee cup with a thump, demanding, 'If he's such a lousy bank manager, why do *you* not change?'

Freyn laughed. 'I was rather waiting for that one,' he said. 'And he isn't a bad bank manager—for me. Of course it helps that I can control him.'

'He's a smarmy, sexist, nasty little man,' Riley retorted. She quivered with distate at the memory of the man's attitude. 'I could have had my re-financing, but the price was rather too high.'

'That way, eh?' Freyn's eyes revealed the distaste this new knowledge provoked. 'Not that I can say I really blame him, but I suspect his approach was just a bit crude.'

'Rude, crude and unattractive,' Riley snapped. 'Just like the man himself, I pity the girls who are forced to work for him.'

Freyn merely shrugged. 'Just as well he went into banking; on your recommendation he'd have made a pretty poor salesman.'

Riley returned the shrug. 'And I'll make a pretty poor logging contractor if I don't spend some more time looking at this forest,' she said. 'Especially if you expect me to try and manage two jobs at once. I have to admit I'm not altogether comfortable with that concept.'

'All you can do is give it a try,' Freyn answered.

He stretched up out of his chair, moving with that fluid grace she was coming to expect from him, and returned a moment later with an aerial photograph of the property with the topographical lines superimposed on it.

'This will give you somewhere to start. We're here, and the ridge we walked this morning is up here. What's left gives you plenty of scope for a nice long hike this afternoon.'

'You're not coming?'

'Why should I?'

'No reason,' Riley replied, hiding the pang of disappointment that his refusal so unexpectedly created. Once she had walked away up the track, however, leaving him behind to attend to some paperwork, she found herself wondering why on earth she should have felt that way.

'Just be sure you're back before dark,' his final words had been. 'I have a dinner date that I daren't be late for, and besides, I've no interest at all in having to come looking for you if you get lost.'

'Thank you very much, I'll try not to,' she had retorted, hiding her outrage at the very suggestion. As if she could possibly get lost with a topographic map to follow!

Still, it was no consolation to return with the fading sun and find Freyn Devereux not even the slightest bit concerned. He was sitting on the stoop of the now darkened house, a warm jumper over his shoulders, staring out into the final pink of the sunset. Riley had the feeling he didn't even notice her arrival.

In the fading light, his strong, bold features seemed cast from pewter. Even his voice, when he finally deigned to speak, had a metallic ring.

'Did you find anything interesting?'

'Trees! Oh, and a place for a landing. I'll get started on that first thing tomorrow.'

'You don't plan on wasting any time, I see.'

'I can't afford to,' she replied, lowering herself to sit beside him, wishing it wasn't quite so dark. She could hear his voice, feel his nearness, but she couldn't see his eyes at all. It made it impossible to judge his mood accurately.

'I thought we'd agreed you'd start off by making some sort of plan? You sound as if you intend to start logging tomorrow.'

'I do,' she replied, voice low and slightly cautious. 'There are plenty of logs near the landing site that can come out while I'm scouting out the rest of the country.'

He said nothing, but she could sense the disapproval.

'I'd like to keep this aerial map, at least for a while,' she said finally, still speaking softly. 'It will be invaluable for sorting out possible access routes.'

'Is that part of the plan, or just to make it faster to get the logs out?' There was a distinctly cold note there, a bitterness she found slightly unexpected.

'Both, in the long run. What I'd like to do is arrange things so that my "snig" tracks can be upgraded to reasonable access roads in due course.'

Again, silence. A brooding, almost palpable silence that hung round them like a tent. Darker than the purpling sky above, and much more ominous.

'You've said nothing about how much compensation you'll need for doing the planning we discussed,' he stated. His voice held accusing notes, as if he was awaiting a rip-off figure.

'I hadn't even thought about it,' Riley said, honestly. 'In fact, I wouldn't even know what figure would be fair. After all, I'll be here anyway, working on the ground. Much of the planning would be just part of my job for Julius.'

'But not all. I expect you'd be spending a reasonable percentage of the time in planning, building access roads, that sort of thing.'

'Yes, but——'

'For instance, you'll more than likely spend time this evening poring over that map to familiarise yourself with it as much as possible,' he said, interrupting her. 'Do you expect to do that for nothing?'

'I——'

He gave her no chance to continue, again interrupting with deliberate rudeness.

'Of course not. Provided that's what you intended. But I rather fancy you'll more likely be out somewhere with the boy-friend, letting work await its proper timing.'

'I hardly see that it's any of your business,' she retorted, growing angry herself now. What was wrong with this man? Why had he suddenly grown sullen and angry?

'It is if I'm paying for it!' was the reply, but before she could say anything he was rising lightly to his feet, one and reaching down for hers, and taking it to help her up before she could think to object.

'Now we'd better be going, or I'll be paying for my own time. We can continue this discussion on the drive back.'

I'd rather not continue it at all, Riley thought, but she allowed herself to be directed into the passenger seat of his shiny station sedan, her axe propped between her feet. And for the journey as far as her home, she was granted her wish. Freyn said nothing as he drove, although she could sense his brooding, angry mood.

Once parked in front of the cottage, he turned the vehicle's interior lights on, and shifted round in his seat to face her. His face was cast in harsh relief by the overhead light, the eyes sunken in shadow, the strong nose appearing more of a hawk's beak than it really was.

'Do you have any objection to working on Saturday?' he asked, voice soft but somehow alive with tension.

'No, but why?' Riley would work seven days a week, especially in the initial stages of this contract, just to restore her slender purse.

'And what's it going to cost you not to work *until* Saturday? Or at least not to cut any timber?'

She got the message then, and curtailed the strong answer that immediately rose to her throat.

'I—well——' She did a swift calculation, then cut the figure in half. The first few days were never terribly productive, and it was already Wednesday night.

When she named the figure, he laughed, but there was no humour in it. Reaching into the glove-box, he withdrew a chequebook and swiftly dashed off a cheque in figures that exactly doubled Riley's amended calculation.

Then he scrawled a name and a bank branch on another piece of paper and handed both over with a grunt of exasperation.

'Tomorrow I want you to use this to open an account with this banker and have a natter with him about sorting out your financial situation,' he said. 'I think you'll find him a good deal more receptive than somebody I could name, whose final dealings with you will be the next item on your agenda when you pay him off and then close your account with a good deal of screaming and yelling.'

At this, Riley tried to interject, but he waved her to silence.

'With luck, when I get there in the afternoon, it will be to have my favourite teller give me chapter and verse about how you threw the money in his face, called him a nasty old man in front of the entire staff and any customers who were handy, and then demanded the strictest of accounting for every cent of interest due you.'

'I—I couldn't do that!'

'What you mean is that you wouldn't. You'd be terrified of the overwhelming applause his staff would give you,' Freyn replied with a chuckle.

'Have it any way you like, but I'm certainly not going to make a public scene about closing out my silly little account with that bank,' she replied. 'And what's more, I can't take this cheque in the first place. It's far too much.'

'How do you know? Nobody's said when you'll get another. And don't be too adamant about refusing to make a scene at the bank, either. I have a feeling that when you see the response you get from the banker I've recommended, you may not feel quite so charitable toward our mutual friend.

'A response I know you're going to influence, although I really don't know why,' she replied. 'Is it just because you fancy yourself as a stirrer?'

'I am going to influence nothing,' he said sternly. 'I will phone to say you're coming and that my cheque is legitimate, and to confirm you'll be logging here on this property. No more than that! The rest is up to you and you alone, but I do recommend the change.'

'I'll think about it,' she replied, cautious now. This was an aspect of Freyn Devereux she had never seen and didn't quite understand.

'You'll *do* it!'

'I'll *think* about it! Damn it, you just can't take over my entire life like this,' Riley cried.

Freyn, who had leaned threateningly close during the swift exchange of hot words, leaned back against the door of the vehicle, a mocking smile on his lips.

'You're a strange woman,' he said. 'Here I offer you

revenge, the easiest you'd ever find, and you just want to argue.'

'I'm not a vindictive person!' Riley exclaimed wearily.

'All women are vindictive.'

In his eyes was the evidence that he believed, fully, in what he said. Some woman, somewhere, had hurt him badly, Riley knew. And he had apparently deserved it, which only made the hurt worse.

She spent the evening poring over his aerial photograph, but all too often she found her vision blurring as her mind wandered. She wondered who had hurt him and in what way. And what had he *done* to deserve it? It was that question that loomed up most often.

CHAPTER THREE

THE next day, following as it did a relatively sleepless night, went almost exactly according to Freyn's plan.

Riley followed his directions, and was duly surprised at the reactions of the banker he'd recommended.

'Look, it isn't the ideal situation, but I'd rather see you at least try to salvage what you have than chuck it all in and take an enormous loss on a sale at this time,' Brent Stewart said. 'You've got work for the equipment, and for yourself, and I think it would be criminal not to take that into account. But—and this is a factor you must consider—I think you'd be mad not to go back and get your degree at the earliest opportunity. I'm sure there is some policy that might even allow you to do it without having to go through the entire final year again.'

'There may very well be,' Riley replied. 'But just now *isn't* the time. I have to consolidate, and thanks to you I can see how to do it now. Once I've got that under control, I'll certainly look at returning to university, but I honestly do think it will be next year at the earliest.'

'As you wish. Just don't throw that option away,' the banker replied. He was a tall, thin, almost cadaverous man whose great saving grace was the smile that lit up his face and totally transformed the overall impression he gave.

'There is one thing I must know,' Riley insisted. 'How much of your—compliance—is due to Freyn Devereux's influence?'

'None. Freyn and I are old mates, and that's all there is to that. You have given me a financial picture that, in my opinion, warrants the actions we're taking. If it didn't, neither Freyn nor anyone else could convince me to get involved.'

'But if you're such mates, why does he bank elsewhere?' Riley asked, and immediately blushed at the realisation that she was enquiring into something that was absolutely none of her business. Brent Stewart was too straightforward for it to matter.

'Friends are friends, and business is business,' he said. 'No sane businessman would deal with a banker who was also a close friend, because it would limit his options too much.'

'Yes, well, I can certainly see that Mr Devereux would never want to do that,' said Riley with feeling.

'I'm glad you do. It wouldn't be wise to get involved in working for him without realising how difficult he can be to get along with sometimes,' the banker cautioned. 'When it comes to stubborn, he'd give the average mule more than just a run for the money.'

'I've noticed,' she replied drily.

Brent laughed. 'You'll more than likely notice it a whole lot more before you finish up,' he said. 'Just don't try and tell me later that you weren't given fair warning, that's all.'

Her encounter with the other banker was almost an anticlimax. She walked in, paid off her loans, closed her account and was gone again within twenty minutes. And all without so much as raising her voice. Instead of the loud noises recommended by Freyn, she chose icy disdain as the appropriate attitude. She replied to the man's agitated questioning with haughty silences, saying only what she wanted to say, when she wanted to say it. Overall, it was a splendidly satisfying experience, she thought. Certainly as much fun as screaming would have been! If Freyn Devereux was truly expecting a report on her performance, he was in for a bit of a disappointment, but that would only serve him right!

By early afternoon she was back at Freyn's forest, aerial map in hand as she continued her reconnaissance. She went home that evening with a substantial part of her planning done, and a much more comprehensive idea of the work that lay ahead.

'I think we'll need both the bulldozer and skidder right from the start,' she told Julius Gunn when she visited him at the sawmill on Friday morning. 'I'm seeing Mr Devereux tomorrow morning, and I hope we'll be ready to start logging by Monday.'

Julius was plesed by the news; wet weather had inhibited work on some other sites where he had access, and he was running short of logs.

Bill Gunn was far less impressed.

'I think you're mad even to consider it,' he said. 'It's one thing to prepare a management plan for this bloke, but to get yourself involved in harvesting the logs—that's madness.'

'I can't imagine why,' Riley replied, hoping he wasn't going to start harping on his old line about marriage. 'I mean, what are you saying? That I can't do the job? You know perfectly well I can. I have!'

'You have not! There's a lot of difference between helping out your Dad when he was alive and trying to step into his shoes entirely. You just don't know what you're letting yourself in for.'

'Oh, I think I've got a pretty good idea,' she asserted. 'And it isn't as if I'm going to be doing it alone. Mackie will be there to help, just as he did with Dad.'

'That's a dandy combination in the bush—a woman and a drunk,' Bill sneered.

'Bill! What an awful thing to say.'

'Well, it's true. How many times did Mackie let your dad down either by not showing up or by being too hung-over to be any damned good to anybody? Just answer that!'

Riley didn't *answer*—she argued.

'Mackie is a good man in the bush,' she avowed. 'He taught me most of what I know, and even Dad used to say he was always learning something from Mackie.'

'He's a geriatric and a soak. The only thing he could have taught your father in recent years was how to drink,' Bill sneered. 'Damn it, Riley, the man's over sixty! He should be retired, not trying to handle the kind of work you've taken on!'

'So name me somebody else I can hire to help,' she retorted. 'You know very well you can't.'

'And wouldn't if I could. Logging is man's work, and I can't think of anybody who'd work for a woman in the bush. Even Mackie wouldn't, given any choice.'

'That's a despicable thing to say!'

'It's the truth.'

'It might be your idea of the truth, but it isn't mine,' Riley countered, her colour high with anger. 'Nor your father's, either, thank goodness.'

'It would be, if he wasn't being blinded by sentiment and the fact this Devereux bloke is being damned difficult about the way he wants his timber handled. This is no job for a woman!'

'I'll make you eat those words, some day!' Riley snapped, and stalked off in high dudgeon before she lost her temper entirely. The nerve! Somehow it was worse having such comments from Bill Gunn, whom she'd always thought of as reasonably open-minded. They had worked together in the bush. He knew what she was capable of.

The worst part was knowing there was just enough truth in Bill's remarks to give cause for worry. It would be difficult, perhaps even impossible, to find another offsider. And it was going to be quite a job, even given the best of help.

'Maybe I have bitten off more than I can chew,' she pondered half-aloud. She repeated the statement silently when she finally tracked Mackie down that afternoon at the Gordon Highlander in Sorell.

The diminutive bushman, not significantly taller than Riley herself, greeted her warmly and with genuine affection, but within minutes it became obvious that he, too, was less than certain about the scale of the job she had taken on. Especially, she realised, his own part in it.

'I'm not getting any younger, and that's a certainty,' he said, peering across his beer glass like some snow-topped gnome.

He was, Riley knew, a very tough sixty-one. He had worked in sawmills or the bush throughout his life, and there was nothing about the tasks before them that he didn't know.

'I suppose you're going to join the Bill Gunn camp of chauvinist pigs, and tell me I shouldn't be doing this at all,' she sighed, suddenly feeling extremely depressed by the breadth of opposition.

'I think you're taking on a big load,' he replied, bright blue eyes peering from beneath a wrinkled brow. 'It's a mighty task, and you're a brave and courageous girl to try it on, but——'

'But I'm a woman, and women don't belong in the bush,' she snapped. 'Damn it, I can drive a bulldozer better than most men, I can work a saw, judge a tree, do anything any man can do—so why is everybody so against me doing it?'

'There's a lot of unemployment about. A lot of men out of work.'

'*I'd* be out of work, without this job.'

'It isn't the same, to some people.'

'Well, it is to me! And unless you're planning to retire on the pension or the dole, it had better be to you, too!

Because if I'm out of it, so are you.'

'Why should you be out of it? You've taken the man's money; you've agreed to do the job. What's stopping you now except for stupid opinions by stupid people?'

'Nothing! And nothing will! I'll do the logging and ram the logs down Bill Gunn's throat!'

'Waste of good timber. And if you're letting young Bill stir you up, I'd have to say I'm disappointed. He's got a lot of growing to do before he's half the man his father is.'

But Riley noticed that Mackie looked furtively round the bar after the words were out. It was one thing to criticise, but Bill's potential as an employer gave the younger man considerable clout that Mackie couldn't match.

'So you'll help me.'

She wouldn't beg, but they both knew the significance of his involvement. Without him, Riley would have to back down. No sane person would go logging on their own; it was a dangerous enough business even with a partner.

'I'll come, if only to see you keep them honest,' Mackie replied. 'And because I need the money and there's damn-all work going elsewhere.'

'You're a love,' Riley laughed. 'And for that I'll even buy you a beer.'

'Two beers,' the old man insisted. 'Not that I need them, but I reckon they might be the last for a bit, if we're to keep Julius Gunn in sawlogs.'

Riley noticed only peripherally the slight hesitation in his watery blue eyes when she proposed a toast to their joint venture. But she definitely noticed how quickly the two beers became four, and then six. Nor could she help but notice the shroud of silence that fell over the bar-room a short time later. It was the typical reaction of locals at the arrival of a stranger, and while

Riley was immediately aware of it, she paid little
attention—until a vaguely familiar voice grated from
above and behind her, the words slashing through the
silence with a ghastly effect.

'Is this how you plan your logging ventures, Miss
Jones?'

'I—well, no,' she stammered, turning to look up, so
very far up, into hazel eyes that seemed dipped in ice.

Freyn Devereux stood like some avenging angel, his
tense attitude hypnotic. Riley found herself wanting to
say more, to explain despite the fact that intellectually
she knew it was none of this man's business.

'It isn't Saturday yet, is it?' she blurted. 'I thought we
were to meet on the property on Saturday morning.'

'We were,' was the caustic reply. 'Although that
shouldn't prohibit us from discussing the situation now.
Presuming, of course, that you're in fit condition to
discuss anything!'

'Steady on!' Riley's composure was recovering
quickly, helped along by the fiery acid of a temper that
seemed to need little prodding from Freyn Devereux's
high-and-mighty attitude.

Freyn's icy glance swept from Riley to Mackie and
back again, and he hardly required further words to
express his attitude. Following that gaze, Riley shivered
inwardly. Mackie certainly wasn't at his most prepos-
sessing.

Then she stiffened, anger flooding through her. What
business was it of Freyn Devereux's anyway? Mackie
was her friend, he wasn't working or supposed to be
working, and if he chose to spend his spare time in the
pub that was nobody's business but his own.

'Are you going to sit down, then? Or stand there
glowering all day?' she said in a voice that challenged
Devereux to either make a verbal fight of it or get out
and leave them alone.

For a moment, she wasn't sure which way it would go. Then Freyn muttered, 'In a minute,' and stalked across to the bar. He returned a moment later with fresh drinks for all of them, and slid into the chair beside her. His manner when she made introductions wasn't exactly friendly, but he seemed to have lost some of the anger she had detected when he had first entered the pub.

Mackie, quick to assess the tension between Riley and Freyn, shook hands with a grin but then immediately retreated into a contrary silence. Freyn, too, seemed determined now to make Riley carry the conversation, and he did so with maddening ease just by looking expectantly at her.

'Was there something you particularly wanted to discuss?' she asked, finding his visual assessment quite disconcerting.

'I understand you think you'll be ready to start logging on Monday,' he replied calmly, making the statement as much a question as anything.

'I was ready to start yesterday,' she replied. 'Or tomorrow, or Monday. I presume by your comment that you've been in touch with Julius Gunn?'

'Just came from there,' he replied, and was silent again with only the faintest hint of a wolfish grin on his lips.

'Looking for me?' She was determined, now, to keep Freyn Devereux from having the upper hand in every aspect of the conversation. If he wanted to be cryptic, she could do it too.

'You wouldn't have been hard to find if I had been,' he replied. 'That truck of yours is pretty noticeable.'

'Really? I wouldn't have thought so.'

'By which you mean you know very well it is.' This time the wolfish grin was obvious. And deliberate.

'Well then, it's served its purpose, since you managed to find me,' she retorted.

'Indeed so. Now, for the bonus prize, do you want to try and guess why?'

'Not really.'

Riley was determined to stay cool, but at this point Mackie deserted her. Declaring it was his shout, he swaggered to the bar, collected fresh drinks, but on his return insisted that he was only in the way, and indeed had a friend he wanted to speak with.

And before Riley could do more than shoot him a furious glare, he was off to the far end of the bar-room, leaving her alone with Freyn Devereux.

'You don't have to look as if you'd been abandoned to the ravages of pirates,' he chuckled, accurately assessing her inner feelings. 'I don't bite—often!'

'But you snarl a lot, and today I'm in no mood for that either,' she admitted. 'So why don't you just tell me why you wanted me, and we can get this over with.'

She pushed the fresh beer idly back and forth across the table, half-concentrating on the damp path it left.

And waited, forever and forever and forever, until finally he spoke.

'I've had to change my plans for tomorrow.'

'You want to meet later, or——'

'Not at all. In fact I'm on my way to Coles Bay now, and likely won't be back until some time Monday. I had asked Julius to pass along the message, since I really didn't expect to run across you.'

'If you've already been to Orielton, this is a pretty strange route to the coast,' Riley mused. 'But then I'm sure you know that.'

'I wasn't sure you'd get the message, so I planned to swing past the property in case you were there,' he replied without turning a hair. The prospect of a forty-kilometre detour obviously hadn't bothered him. 'And now that I've found you, why not have a brief discussion about your plans? I'm sure you're as well prepared now as you would have been tomorrow morning.'

That, she decided, was some concession to his earlier
frosty mood.

'I've got the map in the truck. I'll just get it,' she said,
glad of the opportunity, however brief, to get her
composure back.

Before he might object, she was out of the door and
moving towards where her old truck was parked.

She had the map in her hand and was already turning
back to the pub when her eye caught the shiny reflection
of Freyn's station sedan. With that sight came the
realisation that he was not travelling alone. The woman
who sat in the vehicle, cigarette-holder tipped disdain-
fully out of the open window, was the epitome of blonde
sophistication. More, she was stunningly beautiful.

Riley slowed her pace, drinking in every detail of the
woman as she passed the car. Long, elegantly styled
blonde hair didn't conceal the expensive ear-rings, and
from the little she could see of the woman's dress it was
equally expensive.

But it was the attitude that completed the picture.
This woman was so totally, so obviously conscious of
her own place, her own loveliness, that she was blithely
indifferent to the circumstance of being made to wait in
the car while her man conducted his business.

Riley cast a last quick glance at the blonde, then re-
entered the pub and looked at Freyn Devereux through
new eyes. Where she had earlier been aware only of the
man, now she noticed the quality of his dark suit, the
expensive gleam of wristwatch and ring. It took only an
instant, now that she was looking for it, to realise that
this man wasn't going away for a weekend of business.
Not dressed like that and certainly not with that
particular companion. The blonde, Riley would have
sworn, was the furthest thing from a secretary or any
other sort of business alliance imaginable, which made

it all the more difficult to see why Freyn Devereux would have bothered to drive all the way to his property just to let Riley know he wouldn't be available for a meeting that was hardly of great significance in the first place. Good manners, perhaps. But if he was that insistent on manners he wouldn't be leaving his blonde companion waiting in the car like that.

And whatever his reasons, there was none to explain the way he now looked at Riley herself, his deep hazel eyes roving across her rough work clothing as if it didn't exist, as if he could see right through the jeans and work-shirt to the slender body beneath.

'I—I didn't realise you had somebody waiting,' she said, then could have kicked herself for saying it.

'You noticed. And here I thought you had the only truly distinctive vehicle about the place!' There was just that hint of ill-concealed, scornful laughter in both voice and attitude. Just enough to sharpen her temper, to make her edgy and alert. And cautious.

'This could all wait until next week,' she said. 'It's going to take us a time to build a landing, and bring in the equipment we'll need. There's certainly no massive rush about anything.'

'There is if you want an early start on Monday,' he replied without hesitation. 'Now stop fussing and show me what you've worked out.'

She did so, thankful that she'd carefully marked her proposed roads on the aerial map, and that her notes clearly indicated the reasoning behind each of her proposals. Suddenly she didn't want to be here, didn't want to be discussing business with Freyn Devereux. Not with the knowledge of his woman waiting in the car, waiting with a patience Riley would never have mustered. She just wanted to get this over with, and when he growled his satisfaction she sighed in deep relief.

Too soon.

'I have the feeling you'll be glad to see the back of me,' he remarked with uncanny accuracy. 'Or is it that you'd rather be going with me to Coles Bay this weekend than playing with your logging gear?'

'What a stupid thing to say,' Riley replied, hoping her expression revealed the contempt she wanted to imply. Such thoughts couldn't have been further from her mind—until the very instant Freyn Devereux used his malicious ego to create them. Then, despite her immediate denial, she couldn't help but imagine herself being with him, dressed as exquisitely as the blonde, being pandered to in every way.

'What's the matter? Don't you approve of naughty weekends?'

Damn the man! The question was offered in a voice that sounded almost as if he were serious, but his eyes gave the lie to it all. In their depths was a mocking laughter, a sneer of derision at even the suggestion that a girl with Riley's background would have any place at all in the type of weekend he planned.

Riley caught her temper before it could escape.

'At Coles Bay? Hardly the place I'd choose,' she replied with what she hoped was suitable scorn. 'Unless, of course, one had a particular need for that type of seclusion.'

Then she floundered on, her tongue gaining momentum even as her brain seemed to lose it.

'I suppose it might be a place to avoid a jealous husband, or something like that, but——'

'I do not mess with married women,' Freyn interrupted, and his voice was like a winter wind. Riley felt its blast, but was already formulating the remainder of her remark.

'—then I suppose it also has some cost savings, when compared, say, to West Point, or the casino at

Launceston. But then they are *so* public, and——'

'Careful!' His warning now was more than just a cold voice. She could see the tension in his corded neck muscles, in the long-fingered hand that clenched and unclenched against his thigh.

Riley stopped talking, but it wasn't fear that halted her, it was simply having run out of ideas. Having no personal experience of what he so casually termed a 'naughty weekend' made further comment tricky.

Freyn sat, glaring across the table at her, for what seemed like hours, before the fury faded from his eyes to be replaced by unholy lights of laughter and understanding.

'I think your lack of experience has just let you down, young lady,' he said with a chuckle that grated on her spine. 'Either that, or you've been spending your own naughty weekends with the wrong people.'

'I would expect you to think that,' she snapped back, still floundering for a more acid, challenging reply. This man simply was too sophisticated, too knowing.

'And if I was going to ask *you* away on a weekend I'd best plan on one of the casinos, eh?'

'You'd be better planning on going alone,' Riley retorted, aghast at the inner thrill of speculation he'd created just by the suggestion of such a thing. It was as if somebody had just stroked an ice-cube along her spine, then followed it with a blast of hot air. Riley felt the shudder, and shifted in her seat to cover the movement.

Freyn gave her a wicked, mischievous grin that declared without words how well he could read her reactions, her inner feelings. It was a smile that made her all too aware of her worn working gear, her short, no-nonsense hair-do, her lack of make-up. She suffered the grin, and hated the blonde in Freyn's car with a brief, sudden intensity that swiftly altered to become hatred of the man himself.

'You're certainly full of yourself,' she sneered, fighting against the tears that built up behind her eyes. 'I don't know why you don't just go and spend your weekends with a mirror!'

'Better that than with a chainsaw or a clapped-out truck,' he replied, still with that mocking grin. 'Or is it just that you prefer machinery to men?'

'Infinitely.'

'Your privilege,' he shrugged. 'Perhaps when you're older you'll realise what you're missing.'

Riley returned the shrug, although she didn't believe it possible to feign the confidence he so obviously felt. Especially, she thought, when she couldn't even keep her mind from trying to calculate the age of the exquisite blonde who was waiting for him.

'Don't you think you've kept your—friend—waiting long enough?' she asked at last.

'Trying to get rid of me?'

'Our business is finished.'

'Is it?' And there was something deep within that soft-spoken question, some hidden threat—or promise—that caused Riley's soul to scream out a caution.

'Unless there is something else you wish to discuss,' she insisted, keeping her own voice level now, forcing herself to be cool, calm. She returned his gaze with an icy stare of her own, unconsciously straightening her back, holding her head high. When that brought her breasts into strong relief against the rough material of her shirt, and brought an instant awareness into his glance, she ignored it, fought against showing any reaction at all.

'Whatever there is, it can wait,' he said, rising with swift abruptness. 'I'll see you some time next week, Miss Jones.'

Riley replied in a voice honey-sweet, a voice she hardly recognised as her own.

'Have a good weekend,' she said, and kept from herself the awareness that *he* might, but *she* certainly would not. Freyn Devereux had made certain of that!

Mackie rejoined her only moments after Freyn had left the pub, and the old man's sad blue eyes seemed even more sad than usual.

'You sure do keep some tough company,' he said, not apologising for one moment for having abandoned her as he had. 'Do you really think you're up to working for that man?'

'I don't have much choice, do I?' she replied, the resignation in her voice matching the worry she could see in his deeply-lined face. 'You know as well as I do that there just isn't any other work.'

'You'd be better off on the dole,' Mackie said in a tone that declared he wasn't joking. 'You mark my words, Riley Jones. That man is nobody to mess about with; you'll only get yourself hurt.'

'I'm going to manage his forest, not share his bed!' she cried angrily.

'You reckon? I wonder what he thinks of that,' Mackie replied with a shake of his head. 'I sure got the impression he had more than just logging on his mind, the way you two were slanging at each other.'

'Rubbish!'

Riley didn't want to prolong the conversation, and was spared the need to by the arrival of the trucker her father had always hired to transport the logging equipment from site to site.

It was too good an opportunity to miss, and after several minutes of haggling she had reached an agreement that would see both the bulldozer and skidder delivered to Freyn's property at a price she could afford.

'But it'll have to be tomorrow morning, early,' the man said. 'I'm tied up all day Sunday for servicing and

all next week with some stuff I'm taking to Burnie. If it
was anybody else, I wouldn't even consider working
tomorrow, but I know things have been tough.'

Riley smiled her thanks, bought the man a beer, then
departed for home. The promised early start tomorrow
meant a lot of last-minute planning.

She didn't get to bed until late, had considerable
trouble sleeping, but managed to be prepared for
loading when the truck arrived at dawn. By noon, she
and Mackie were waving goodbye to the trucker, their
heavy equipment safely on the ground and ready for
work.

During her walking expeditions, Riley had already
selected the tree that would serve as the bedlog for her
landing. It was an enormous old blue gum, half burned
out at the base and riddled with rot. Totally unfit for any
conventional timber usage, it was perfectly situated for
the job she had in mind.

Half an hour's work with the loading blade of the
skidder and she had cleared the light undergrowth from
the landing site. It took them less time than that to drop
the huge tree, lop off the top and drag it into position.

Riley took the bulldozer then, and started pushing her
'snig' track network, leaving Mackie to find and
position two skid poles across the ends of the bedlog so
that he could fill the space between with packed earth.

Then they went off to begin felling the first trees,
working into a stand of tall, straight, stringy barks in a
deliberate pattern that made for quick, efficient
movement of the logs once they were down and topped.

By mid-afternoon they had two truckloads dragged
down to the landing and Riley was prepared to call it a
day. She knew that Mackie had stayed too long at the
pub the night before, and her muscles had protests of
their own.

'I've got soft!' she grunted, stretching her arms high

and swinging them as she tried to ease the soreness in her shoulders and wrists.

'You'll toughen up quick enough,' the old man replied. 'I'd give it a rest tomorrow. You could do yourself an injury if you keep at things too hard.'

'If I rest tomorrow, I won't be able to move by Monday,' Riley replied with assurance. 'And you won't be much better—it's a while since you did this much work.'

'All I need is to leave the grog alone tonight,' he replied with a grin. 'I should have left last night when you did, but—well . . .'

She laughed, knowing he would more than likely be back in the pub tonight. And knowing she certainly would not be. 'I reckon we won't do too much tomorrow,' she said. 'Just finish getting the bark off these logs and see what else is handy.'

'Might as well do all we can,' said Mackie. 'The weather can't hold good for ever, and if we can't be logging when it gets wet, then we'll need a good stockpile of logs we can deliver.'

'First load on Monday, then.'

Sunday's weather turned out to be perfect. Clear skies and brilliant sunshine combined with cool temperatures to make a day ideal for hard physical work.

Riley found it took until noon to stretch the kinks out of muscles objecting to the regimen; after a leisurely lunch including two cups of strong tea, she felt truly fit and surprisingly energetic.

'There's that one big gumtop just along the road there,' she said to Mackie. 'I'd like to get him out of the way and dragged up here while the track's dry, so that I can remake the road if I have to.'

He nodded his agreement, then indicated that he would continue the job of barking the logs already assembled. Riley picked up her saw and walked downhill along the track they would use to haul out the logs.

The tree was a good one, sufficiently large that the resultant sawlog would make a truckload all by itself. The safest way to fell it would mean the crown would land square on the track, but that would be no real problem. After topping, she could use the skidder to shift the unwanted material and then get the log up to the landing without damaging the road very much at all.

The first part of the operation, cutting in the deep, V-shaped *face* that would determine the direction of fall, went like clockwork. Riley had already surveyed the forest giant from every viewpoint, judging the slight angle of the tree, the relative mass of overhanging limbs, the direction and strength of the light afternoon breeze.

Force of habit, however, caused her to double-check before she got stuck into the main cut that would leave nothing of the tree but a massive stump. She stood, peering upward, unable to dislodge the feeling of awe and the slight twinge of pity that such a magnificent specimen should so easily succumb to the power of the modern chain-saw. Then she began her main cut.

It was perfect. The tree yielded to the saw, finally teetering with a creaking groan of submission and then thundering down to thump squarely where she'd planned.

Hopping up on the trunk, she began pacing towards the crown, measuring the length as she walked. It wasn't until she reached the first major branch that she saw the vehicle stopped only metres from the wide-spread crown, a shiny, familiar, but unexpected vehicle.

And beside it, glowering at her, Freyn Devereux!

CHAPTER FOUR

'YOU'RE early!' The words emerged in a squeak. Half a minute earlier, Riley thought, would have been too early *and* too late. Fatal!

She forced herself to meet his angry glare, fighting to repel the nausea that surged through her at the thought of such an accident.

He said nothing. Even when Riley could bear it no longer, and knelt to place the saw carefully against a balancing branch, fighting against the trembles in her legs.

But his silence had better effect than anything he might have said. It served to give her a slight breathing space, a chance to regain her composure. With it came the realisation that he must surely be as much to blame for the near-miss as she had been.

'It's a bit dangerous, driving into a logging area like that,' she found herself saying—and could have cursed at how puerile the comment must sound to a man who has almost been crushed by a falling tree! The very narrowness of the shave again forced shivers through her. How could she have been so careless? Of course she hadn't been expecting Freyn, and she had known exactly where Mackie was and what he would do under any circumstances. But there was an element of carelessness in felling a tree across a navigable track, and she had ignored that entirely.

'It's a good thing I wasn't any damned earlier!' Freyn replied, and there was no sign of fear in those hostile eyes. Only frightening, icy anger.

'Well, it would have been a better thing if you'd have

used your eyes to see with and your ears to listen!' Riley
shot back. 'Surely you could hear the saw?'

'Of course I could. But I hardly expected you to be
dropping trees all over the roads!' he retaliated.

'*One* tree. On *one* road.'

'And damned near on *my* car! But then of course you
weren't expecting any cars, were you?'

'Well, of course not. You told me yesterday you'd be
gone until Monday some time. Nobody else has any
business up here but us, and maybe Julius Gunn if you
want to get really technical. And Julius would have
more sense than to drive that close to an area where he
could hear a saw!'

'I'm glad somebody in this operation has a bit of
sense,' he retorted, not moving from his angry stance
beside the open door of the car. 'I'm just sorry it couldn't
have been you, that's all!'

Riley was now fully recovered—however temporar-
ily—from the shock of the near-accident. And with the
recovery came a blistering wave of anger that bore no
relationship to the circumstances or her own responsibility. It was this man, this man who seemed always
deliberate in his attempts to belittle her, to sneer at her
and do his level best to put her in the wrong.

'I'm just sorry you weren't thirty seconds earlier,' she
snarled, voice spitting cat-like in her rage. 'Now, if
you'll excuse me, I'll finish topping this tree so that I can
clear the road. Then you can drive your *damned* car
wherever it is you want to go!'

'Without any apology, of course.'

His voice had gone strangely soft as she reached
down for her saw. Now it was a voice that screamed
caution in a whisper.

Riley paused, half-kneeling. She felt the warnings in
his tone, felt them trickle like ice-water down her spine.

Despite her anger, she knew he was right, at least in part.

'Oh, all right, I apologise,' she said then, first straightening to look him squarely in the eye. 'There was a risk there and I should have planned for it.'

'And I should have waited somewhere safer, instead of driving right into the middle of things,' was the absolutely astonishing response.

Riley simply stared, unable to believe her ears. Thirty seconds before, they had been in the middle of a vicious slanging match; now he was apologising.

Even stranger, the hostile gleam was gone from those intense hazel eyes. They still weren't what she would ever call friendly, but the bitter anger was gone, the coldness was gone.

'I—you didn't have to say that. But thank you.'

'I just thought it would be safer to have some sort of truce under way before you fired up that machine again. It would make a frightening weapon,' he said, with just a hint of a grin. 'Now do you want me to shift my car, so you can get on with whatever comes next?'

'Yes, please. About twenty feet back will be enough,' Riley answered. She watched, mildly bewildered, as he meekly obeyed. Then she switched on the chain-saw and yanked at the starter rope with practised skill. The saw roared into life; she turned her back on Freyn and began to undercut the log as a prelude to lopping the crown.

There was an immense feeling of satisfaction when, a few minutes later, the lopping was completed without incident. Riley turned off the saw, set it down carefully with the blade resting in the heap of fresh sawdust, and drew a deep breath before once again turning around.

'That was nicely done.'

A compliment? She wondered idly if he had any real idea of the complexity of her work, thought about that before replying, and decided he just might.

'A good tree, that one,' she said. 'It'll go maybe thirteen metres—a load all by itself.'

'So what next?'

'I'll get Mackie to come down with the skidder and take it back up to the landing, shove the top off the road and bring the dozer down to tidy up afterwards. That's the only tree we'll be taking down here below the landing, so I want to put the road in top condition while things are still dry.'

'I'll walk up with you,' he said abruptly. 'Even carry the saw, if you like!'

Now there was a hint of schoolboy mischief in his tone, almost as if he were offering to carry her books. Riley felt a mixture of pleasure and stark caution, a curious mixture of emotions that unsettled her.

'I'll manage, thanks,' she said, and picked up the heavy saw herself. Then she walked towards the landing, all too aware that Freyn Devereux was right behind her, that he was watching her long strides, relentless in his assessment of her as a woman. Maybe it should have been a compliment, but it served more to put her on edge, to worry her.

She said nothing more to Freyn until she had directed Mackie to his part of the work. Once the skidder had roared off down the track, she clambered into the truck cabin and found the half-full thermos of tea.

'Want some?' she asked, reaching up to take off her hard hat and scrub her fingers through the short, damp hair. It wasn't warm enough for her to be sweating, she thought, and put it down to the closeness of the near-miss accident.

'Thanks, I will,' Freyn replied. With scant regard for his soft corduroy trousers, he eased himself down to squat on a section of cut-off log-butt beside the landing. Even as he accepted the tea, his eyes were moving

around the site, and as she followed his gaze Riley
realised how incredibly messy it must seem to him.
There were tatters of bark everywhere, a few small trees
flattened by the back-and-forth gyrations of the
skidder, and the growing stockpile of thick logs.

Did he realise, she wondered, just how much more
messy it was going to get? In a few weeks the whole
landing site would be awash with discarded bark. And
if it rained, the ground would quickly be churned into a
morass of mud and bark and more mud.

Freyn sipped at his tea, saying nothing. And Riley,
when she nervously broke the silence, found herself
asking, 'Your weekend didn't go as . . . planned?'

It was shockingly impudent, and obviously as much a
surprise to Freyn as it was to herself. Had she really said
that?

'I suppose you could put it that way,' he replied after a
frankly disconcerting glance at Riley. 'Something came
up that forced it into being cut short, anyway.'

'I see.'

'Do you? Before you get any more curious about my
private life, just have a thought about what curiosity did
to the cat!'

'I didn't mean to pry.'

But she had, subconsciously or otherwise. And worse,
he knew it as well as she.

'Neither did the cat,' he replied grimly. 'Why don't
you just come out and ask if I wouldn't have been
more—successful—if I'd taken you to the casino as you
wanted?'

'I—you——' She sat there, stunned with amazement
at the sheer audacity. Her mouth opened and shut, but
still she couldn't find a coherent word of reply.

'And of course the thought of such a weekend never
so much as crossed your innocent little mind, did it?'

Oh, the sneering mockery! The smug smile when her

flaming face betrayed her with an admission that needed no words!

He hadn't moved, but suddenly he was there with her, one arm reaching to pull her close as his lips descended. Riley was caught with her thermos in one hand and her entire defence system awry. He was kissing her before she even thought to fight him.

His kisses were first gentle, merely token explorations as his mouth sought her lips, teasing, searching the contours of her response. But as her lips parted with an eagerness she couldn't have imagined, his kisses became bolder, more insistent. One hand reached out to pluck the thermos from her nerveless fingers, and without releasing her lips, he reached out and set it on the bonnet of the truck. Then his arms were firm at her waist again, the strong fingers warm as they explored the softness there.

Riley's own hands went first against his shoulders in a futile bid for freedom, a freedom she didn't really want but knew she must fight for. Then her resistance faltered as the play of muscle beneath her fingers seemed to radiate its own message to her hands.

Her arms searched around his neck, fingers exploring through the thickness of his hair, the more compulsive in their search as his lips dipped down to follow the pulse in her throat. She felt as if she must explode, as if her body was floating, her mind askew with colour and fire and the madness of sensations until now unknown, not even dreamt of.

When his lips returned to her mouth, her lips parted to welcome his kiss. When they shifted lower, parting the front of her work-shirt in a fiery search for her breasts, she felt the mad desire to undo the buttons, anything to ease the passage of such ecstasy. She could hear her own voice, as if from some great distance, moaning, sighing, crooning with pleasure, and she wanted to scream when his fingers slipped beneath her shirt, running a path of fire up her ribs to culminate in an experienced, maddening assault on her breasts.

In some dim recess of her brain, she was conscious of the far-off roaring of the skidder, and she tried to focus on that, tried to find some anchorage for the tiny remnants of sanity.

'No . . . oh, no!' The words could have been a scream, or they could have been a silent whisper inside her head. Riley didn't know, but the fingers now exploring inside the front of Freyn's shirt balled into a fist, a fist without strength or direction, but a fist for all that.

As if he sensed her return from the brink of utter abandonment, he suddenly released her.

'So much for curiosity,' he growled, in a voice still alive with the passion they had both felt, but there was also a note of mockery there, a gleam of triumph in his eyes that was a catalyst to Riley's confused emotions.

Where there had been passion there were now only the flickering embers of frustration; tempestuous joy had turned to stone.

'How dare you?' She stepped back, trembling, her fingers searching for a weapon.

'Oh, don't be childish,' he retorted. 'It wasn't the first time you've been kissed, and I'm sure it won't be the last, so stop making such a big thing of it.'

The calm logic of his remark served only to make her more angry, not least because he was probably all too right.

'Kissed? More like assaulted, wouldn't you say?'

'Hardly assault!' And he was laughing, now. Not outwardly, but she could see the laughter in his eyes, feel it in the rich tones of his voice. 'Just a small demonstration, so that if you decide to get curious about my extra-curricular activities again you'll have some point of reference.'

'I couldn't care less about your "extra-curricular activities", or any other kind you might have,' Riley snapped back. 'And you can keep your demonstrations to yourself while you're at it!'

'Ah, but experiences shared are so much more rewarding,' he grinned, and there wasn't so much as a hint of remorse, a suggestion of guilt.

'Well, save your sharing for somebody who appreciates it,' Riley said. 'I can happily do without.'

'And here I thought you were enjoying it,' was the laughing rejoinder. 'Unless of course that response was only an act.'

Riley gritted her teeth. Damn him for his knowing ways, for his easy, casual acceptance of his ability to turn her emotional equilibrium inside out!

'Not denying it? That's a bit surprising from you, Miss Jones.'

She refused to be drawn further. It wouldn't matter what she said, Riley knew. He had the upper hand, and he was all too aware of it.

They stood there, less than a metre apart, staring at each other like strange, stray cats, so totally absorbed in their verbal and mental conflict that Mackie almost ran them both down when he arrived with the huge log in tow. Obviously expecting them to be aware of their surroundings, he sped into the landing area and had to slow visibly to keep from hitting them.

Riley leapt backwards in sudden alarm, but was caught up in mid-air by Freyn's strong arm circling her waist as he lifted her in behind her truck.

Mackie, his surprise evident in the startled glance he shot them as he passed, continued his progress to the log dump. Riley, struggling against the iron grip round her waist, could feel the colour rising to her face.

What would the old man think of that performance? she wondered. And could almost hear the words of him relating the experience to his bar cronies.

'Riley Jones and that Devereux fellow, squared off like two stray dogs in the middle of the landing. Never so much as heard me coming, they didn't. Damned near flattened them both, and me dragging a log so big it made a load all by itself. Never saw anything so funny . . .'

'Put me down!' she cried, ignoring the fact that Freyn had already done so, and was only steadying her.

Mackie, having positioned the log and released his snig chain, turned off the rumbling monster, leaving time suspended in a silence that felt weird, unreal. Freyn had released her without a word, but he stood only inches away, and she could feel the heat of him; her body still retained the pressure of him. She felt as if he hadn't really let go at all.

She watched as Mackie descended from the machine, her mind whirling with criticisms she knew she daren't voice. It wasn't his fault, but because of the embarrassing situation she wanted to scream at him, to strike out. Even though she knew only too well that her real target should be the tall, russet-haired man beside her.

'You two gone deaf or something?' asked Mackie with a cautious, almost timid smile. It was as if he *knew*.

Riley felt like crawling under a board, slinking off to hide somewhere. But she steeled herself, forcing into her voice a calm she didn't feel.

'We weren't paying attention, that's for sure!' But when she tried to follow up with a casual laugh, it emerged as a croak.

'All the more reason to save the rest of our discussion for another time and a safer place,' Freyn said then, his own voice showing—maddeningly!—no concern whatsoever. 'So can I suggest you stop by the house when you're finished here today? I won't keep you long, but there are one or two things yet to clear up.'

Riley, still far too aware of his closeness, could only nod an acceptance, much as she felt like refusing.

Then Mackie ventured a comment that made any refusal impossible, and Riley could cheerfully have strangled him for it.

'We're almost done here, anyway, so why not go down now?' he asked. 'I can finish up and I'll bring the truck down and collect you on the way by.'

Now there was no room for refusal, but plenty of room to make her feelings obvious as she and Freyn walked downhill towards his station sedan. Riley walked in silence, not looking at him, not even acknowledging his presence. When they reached his vehicle, she got into it without giving him any opportunity to play the gentleman by opening her door.

There was a twinge of concern that her jeans might be harbouring oil or grease that could stain the immaculate interior of the car, but she quickly ignored that. Serve him right, she thought.

When they reached the tiny cottage, it appeared Freyn had accepted her icy mood, though he certainly didn't seem particularly bothered about it. He marched into the cottage ahead of her, sat down at the table, and waited silently until she, too, sat down.

'I'll be away for a while. You'll maybe need these, so you'd best have them,' he said without preamble. 'Key for the main gate, key for the cottage. My office and home phone numbers.'

He handed over the two keys and single slip of paper, but Riley made an immediate attempt to hand back the cottage key.

'I have no need for this,' she said.

She was ignored.

'You may find a need for better first-aid supplies than you carry, or more of them. You could find yourself caught in a storm, in which case this place will be a damned sight more comfortable than the cab of your truck.'

'I said I have no need for it,' she protested.

'Who knows, you might want to come up for a naughty weekend!' he continued, ignoring the protest as if she hadn't spoken. 'I realise it isn't up to the standard of the state's casinos, but it is private.'

'That's uncalled-for!'

'Just a suggestion.' And now he was smiling, if you could call it a smile. Riley bristled. He was deliberately taunting her, and they both knew it.

'Just be sure you check with me first, in case I have plans in that direction myself,' he added, the grin widening as Riley's eyes narrowed in angry disbelief.

'My God! I suppose next you'll be suggesting we might get together and have a foursome!' she snarled, not asking him, but stating the insult as a foregone conclusion.

'Not a chance,' he replied firmly. 'If you and I ever get it together, my dear Miss Riley, it will be purely on a one-to-one basis. You have my word on that!'

'I can imagine what your word would be worth,' Riley snapped, then paused, open-mouthed, as the import of her reply sank in. Open mouth, insert feet, she thought.

Freyn's laughing reply was no help at all.

'Would you like to re-phrase that?' he chuckled. 'You sound as if you're not sure whether you want me to honour the promise or not.'

'*Not!*'

'Could have fooled me.'

'I doubt,' she said in her iciest voice, 'if that would be terribly difficult.'

Freyn laughed, and there were undertones of his immense self-assurance in the laughter.

'A lot of people have tried to fool me,' he replied. 'And some of them have even managed it, an admission

I'm sure will surprise you. Although to be fair, not too many have been women.'

And there was something in the way he said it that led Riley to the assurance that 'not too many' could as easily have been said as 'one', but it had been that one woman who had left Freyn Devereux with a lifetime wariness where the opposite sex was concerned.

It was a sobering thought, considering the confusion of her own reactions to the man. She was totally off balance, swinging from angry hatred to a sensual, physical and mental attitude that made him seem too attractive by half. The one thing certain, however, was that he was far too experienced for her to handle, and even to try would be a dangerous emotional risk.

'Well, I have no interest in fooling you,' she began, only to be interrupted.

'Just want to fool around?' He laughed again at the immediate effect his words created.

Riley was not as amused.

'I think I'll wait for Mackie outside, if it's all the same to you,' she said soberly. 'I've had about as much of this as I can take.'

'What you have, dear Miss Jones, is no sense of adventure. Absolutely none,' Freyn chuckled. 'And what bothers me even more is that you have about that much sense of humour.'

'My sense of humour is my own damned business,' Riley snapped, and turned for the door. She was doubly angry now, the feeling intensified by an inexplicable tenderness she had felt for him only moments before. Why she should have felt such a thing, she couldn't imagine. If Freyn Devereux had been hurt by a woman—any woman—he had almost certainly deserved it.

'I could make it my business,' he said, and the words were strangely soft, strangely alluring. Frighteningly so!

'*My* business is logging, thank you,' she replied, and cringed, inwardly, at how prissy that sounded. 'Yours— what *do* you do, anyway?'

'I'm in computers, among other things. Mostly computers, though. Does that surprise you?'

It didn't, because she was sure she had heard Julius Gunn mention it at some time. But Riley wouldn't admit that, not now.

'Only slightly,' she replied. 'I wouldn't have figured you for the mathematical type.'

He laughed.

'There's more to computers than maths,' he said. 'In fact I sometimes think I should have taken languages at university; it might have served me better now.'

'What did you take?'

Riley was genuinely interested now, her earlier hostility forgotten, or nearly so, at this unexpected opportunity to know more about this unusual man.

'Maths, of course. And computer sciences, although to be honest I found the state of the art was changing so fast that I was well ahead of my instructors for most of the time.'

'And your—aunt? The woman who had this place before you?'

'She was a naturalist, albeit an amateur one. Better than a lot of professionals, though, if I do say so myself. She knew what she knew because she lived in the field, not just because she read about it.'

'She must have been a remarkable person,' Riley said.

'What makes you say that? You didn't know her—or did you?'

'I feel I did, if you can understand that. It's this house, I suppose. There's nothing of you here, or of me or anyone else. Just her! And you've only to look around to see that she was very tidy, very involved in her life. How old was she when she . . .'

'Eighty-six going on nineteen.' He said it with a smile of reminiscence, a slow, genuine, very soft smile that told Riley more than anything he could say how much he had felt for the woman who had lived in this tiny cottage.

'She came to this property as a girl, younger than you,' he continued. 'Her husband, my uncle, was a family black sheep, always involved in land speculation, land development and clearing. In fact, I'm surprised this property isn't honeycombed with bulldozer tracks; every other place he ever set foot in was.'

Now Riley could laugh.

'I don't see what's so funny about that,' Freyn remarked, meeting her laughter with a frown and a growl.

'You don't see very much at all.' She managed to get that much out, then burst into laughter again.

He scowled, but said nothing, only waiting with growing impatience until she had finished.

'Computer sciences and maths might be all right in town,' she said, her bosom still heaving with laughter only just held in check. 'But if you're going to do much with this place, you'd better go back and take a course in bushmanship or something.'

'Explain!'

She paused, the laughter under better control as she considered the frostiness of his attitude. Riley knew that nobody much likes being laughed at, and Freyn would be even more sensitive than most, she reckoned.

'The property *is* filled with old tracks,' she explained, keeping it simple, direct. 'You can't see much of them now; they're heavily overgrown. But they're there, certainly. Everywhere!'

In fact, she had remarked to Mackie earlier that day about the maze of old tracks, so overgrown as to be virtually invisible to anyone not skilled in the bush. For Riley and Mackie—both well used to seeking out access to the biggest trees, the easiest routes—the old tracks stood out like highways.

'Are you having me on?'

'Certainly not. And if you don't believe me, ask Mackie when he gets here,' she replied.

'And why is it that you can see these tracks and I can't?'

'Well, because I guess that's one thing that hasn't changed since the days when they logged with bullocks, I suppose. Easy access, terrain, ease of movement—they're all just as important now as then. The old-timers who built the tracks I'm talking about were looking for the same things I do when I'm planning snig tracks, so it's logical enough that most of the ones I've looked at so far have already been used before by somebody.'

'How long ago?' The expression on his face told her he was genuinely interested now, no longer angry.

'Long before I was born, that's for sure,' she replied. 'Probably even before you were born. Just before or maybe during the war, I'd reckon. Or maybe during the twenties or early thirties, with bullocks. They took some big trees out of here, in places—much bigger than those here now.'

'And you can pick these tracks up when you're just walking through the scrub?'

'Sometimes, although more often than not from up on the bulldozer. It isn't really that hard, once you know what to look for.'

'Hmmm,' he muttered. 'Yes, I can see that. Knowing what to look for is half the battle in most things.'

The curious, half friendly, half speculative look that he shot her after that remark cast a slight shiver up Riley's spine.

She wasn't sorry to hear the roar of the arriving utility

to end the conversation. All her instincts told her it had been about to take a new tack, and that it might have been in a direction she'd be better off avoiding.

Especially when, despite Mackie's presence, Freyn looked very much like he could be giving serious consideration to kissing her again before she left.

He must have sensed her instinctive pulling away, however, because, instead of kissing her, he merely grinned wickedly and reached out to shake her hand. Very much man-to-man was the gesture. Overly so; it was exaggerated almost to the point of being offensive.

'I'll see you in a week or two,' Freyn smiled, his voice soft and yet clear over the sound of the truck engine.

Mackie, having stepped out to relinquish the driving seat to her, also came in for a handshake, but it was to Riley alone that Freyn's final words were directed. And since he spoke so softly she could hardly hear him, only part of the message came though.

'Don't drop any trees on anybody.'

She got that part all right, and the instinctive surge of guilt and anger pushed the rest of the remark into a kind of limbo until they were nearly half-way home. Only then did she realise that his final words might have been—must have been—'especially on yourself'.

The realisation hit her like a bombshell, for reasons she couldn't explain. Mackie was justifiably startled when she almost ran off the road.

'What was that all about?' he demanded, eyes wide with apprehension.

'I guess you were right about today. We should have given it a miss,' Riley replied. 'I'm just tired, that's all.'

His grunt could have meant anything, but somehow she didn't think it meant he believed her. Only that he wasn't going to pry.

And he didn't. The next two weeks simply flew past as they were blessed with a spate of non-stop good

weather, easily worked timber, and not a single
mechanical problem. Within days they had established
a solid teamwork, each with a specific end of the work
to handle and the ability to work at peak efficiency
without constant chatter. It was, Riley quickly realised,
the way her father had always been able to work with
Mackie. The old bushman knew his timber and he knew
his work. He could judge the girth of a tree from fifty
yards away, could mark and establish the direction of
fall with deceptive ease, and correct it just as easily.

And best of all, he'd given up the grog.

- They had set their pace at just over a truckload of logs
per day, and usually exceeded that margin by one or two
logs without difficulty. Even so, Riley had sufficient
time to continue planning her network of tracks, and to
spend an hour or so checking out future development
areas, regrowth stands and young timber.

It was easy to see where the short-term programme
would lead; there was easily a year's supply of sawlogs
without getting into the steeper, less accessible areas.
But in the long term, the planning was nowhere near as
obvious. Given a totally free hand, Riley would have
spent a bit of time searching out some reliable firewood
hawker. Properly directed, such activities would clear
out the rubbish timber, thinning the bush to give the
new young trees and better regrowth a chance.

The biggest problem would be one of supervision,
because—as she knew only too well—nobody got rich
cutting firewood, and there was always the tendency to
cut corners, take short-cuts, or knock off potentially
good timber because it was handiest.

She and Mackie, with neither having a family to
support, were able to make a respectable living from
their work, but somebody wood hawking would have
things somewhat tougher.

'Still, it's what should be done here,' she said to her

partner one day at lunch. The old man was sceptical.

'Only if you could find somebody reliable, and you know how hard that could be. I reckon you'd best concern yourself with our own work, and let this Devereux bloke make his own arrangements, if that's what he wants.'

'Who knows *what* he wants?' Riley replied. 'After being so determined to know every detail when we started, he's apparently decided to just ignore us. Probably lost interest already.'

'Not that man,' Mackie said bluntly. 'He's not the type to lose interest in anything he's set his mind to. I'd be warned by that, if I were you.'

'Meaning?'

'Meaning just what you think it means. If your father were alive, I'd say nothing, but——'

'No buts, I'm a big girl now and I can handle my own affairs,' Riley interrupted.

'You're the boss,' Mackie acknowledged, and Riley had to force herself to try and ignore the stubborn, almost bitter tone.

'Just see that you remember it,' she replied lightly, throwing him her warmest smile to show she wasn't serious, to assure him of how much she needed his advice, his help, his knowledge. In respect of everything but Freyn Devereux. Where Freyn was concerned, there was nothing Mackie could do that would be of any assistance whatsoever.

'Oh, I'll remember all right. Just see that *you* do, when the time comes,' he replied, then turned away before she could seek further enlightenment about such an enigmatic statement.

The exchange put a sort of damper on the rest of the day, and although the work went as well as usual, Riley found herself thinking back to Mackie's unusual attitude. By late afternoon, she had resolved to bring up the subject during the drive back to the mill, but only minutes before they were due to knock off, that resolution was killed by the arrival of the very man they had been discussing.

Freyn walked into the landing area unannounced, moving nonchalantly along the track in his usual countryman's gear.

Riley would, at one time, have smiled inwardly at the tweed jacket, the soft corduroy trousers and the expensive, hand-made leather boots that must have been supremely comfortable, however impractical for any real bush work.

But now when she noticed him, she was struck only by how the clothing suited him, how totally at ease he looked, how comfortable. There was just so much total self-assurance. Freyn Devereux could have arrived at the landing wearing a dinner suit and still exuded that astonishing confidence and masculinity.

As he approached her, she found herself noticing his hands. Not work-roughened like her own, or—far more so—Mackie's, but nonetheless strong, competent hands, capable hands. She sensed that, given the need, Freyn could easily handle any manual labour he had the skills for, and without any sense of inadequacy if he didn't have the skills. He would, she thought, simply set out to learn them.

The truck was loaded when he arrived, and Mackie was off skidding in the final log of the day. When that was barked, they would be away. Or would have been.

'You've been moving right along, I see,' Freyn said when he was close enough to speak.

'We've had good weather.' It was all Riley could think of. The swift sexual assessment in his eyes, the way his glance flickered up and down her body, seemed to take her breath away, to numb her mind.

'Looks more like good, hard work,' he replied.

Riley took a strange delight in the implied compliment. Her back straightened slightly and she saw the fire in his eyes flash as the gesture thrust forward her breasts and tautened the muscles of her long, slender throat.

Despite the steep climb from the house, he was breathing easily, although she fancied she could see his nostrils flare at the sharp scent of crushed eucalyptus bark that pervaded the landing area.

'You've had no problems, obviously.'

'Not a single one.' Except, she thought, for having missed him, despite not realising it until now. She gave herself a mental shake. She had *not* missed him, she could not miss him, and she had better not even think of such things.

It worked for an instant. Until he smiled that slow, warm grin that massaged a path of rhythmic fire up her spine. But then Mackie arrived to intrude on that instant of special intimacy, the skidder roaring into the pleasant silence. Freyn greeted him with a wave, then turned his attention once again to Riley.

'You must be about done for today. Walk back down to the house with me, and Mackie can pick you up when he's finished.'

It was a curious mixture of appeal and command, not that Riley had any intention of objecting. It was as if she had merely been awaiting the request, her subconscious mind already priming her mouth for a 'yes'.

She turned to collect her jacket and gloves, and as she did so, Freyn stepped over to the now silent skidder and lifted himself up to the high cab to speak with her partner.

But as they walked away together down the track, he lapsed into a characteristic silence, and neither of them spoke during the journey to the small cottage.

Freyn opened the door to a flood of warm air; he had

obviously been here long enough to get the fire going and warm the interior, which gave Riley a moment's curiosity.

'Coffee?' He was already switching on the electric kettle. From the way it quickly burbled to life, she could tell it had been in use before during the afternoon.

He stood there, pensively watching the light spurts of steam, then poured the hot water over spoonfuls of instant coffee and set them on the table before saying anything else.

'What else have you got to report? Any further progress on a long-term plan?'

'I have a few ideas that warrant talking about,' she replied, suddenly shy, less than secure.

'So why not sit down, start on your coffee, and we'll do that? The chair doesn't bite, you know?' He grinned at the obvious pleasure of having yet again caught her off guard.

Riley didn't reply, but she did sit down. Her fingers laced themselves around the warm cup at the same time as her boots tucked round the chair rungs, as if seeking some firm support.

Freyn seated himself opposite her, eyes hooded in the shafts of late-afternoon sunlight that cascaded through the window beside him. Riley thought that he settled himself with the grace of some great cat, and his eyes now held the same type of unblinking, penetrating stare. Again, she was all too conscious of her worn work-clothing, of the sawdust chips in the folds of her shirt, in her thick, short hair. There was bound to be a smudge on her forehead where she had casually wiped away the perspiration during the day, and her fingernails were grimy and chipped. She shifted uneasily and passed a hand through her hair.

'I don't know why you persist in being so touchy about your appearance,' he said then, picking up her thoughts accurately. 'There's nothing to be ashamed of in working for a living.'

'I should hope not!'

'Well then, stop playing Cinderella after the ball. When I want you to do that, I'll show up with a glass slipper!'

'It wouldn't fit.'

Riley had meant the comment to be light, diversive. But somehow it came out tinged in bitterness, coloured by her memory of the beautiful blonde she had seen with Freyn, by thoughts of immaculate hair, perfect fingernails.

'Hey, now! That doesn't sound like the girl I left behind,' said Freyn, his voice mingling concern and a successful attempt at lightness where she had failed. 'I thought you said you'd been having a good run up here.'

'We have.'

'Then why so glum?'

'I'm not glum. Just a bit tired, perhaps.'

She smiled brightly, hoping that would steer him off the track of logic. To have him think she was concerned about her appearance only on his behalf would be too embarrassing for anything.

Picking up her coffee, she turned away from his gaze, focusing her own eyes to where the sun was gradually sinking into a bank of cloud. Freyn let her slide into her silence, and although she was conscious of him watching her watching the sky, it wasn't an obtrusive observation. Still, she could tell when his eyes left her face as he also gazed out of the window.

She was only dimly conscious also of the dull thunder as Mackie eased the heavy load down the track. Until the thunder became a roar that should have stopped and didn't!

'He isn't stopping!'

Riley was on her feet and through the door, but only

in time to see the vehicle rock down the road, the red flag in the end of the longest log waving a mocking farewell.

'You arranged that!'

She turned to find Freyn beside her, watching the truck depart without any shred of conscience or dismay.

'I said I'd drive you back. We have to talk anyway, and you'll be more comfortable with me.'

'I'd be more comfortable making my own decisions!' Riley cried. 'What right do you think you've got to be ... to be ...'

'What right do I need to offer you a lift? You're getting paranoid or something, Miss Jones.'

'And probably with good reason,' she snarled, suddenly only too aware of being alone with him, of *having* to be alone with him.

'Such as ...?'

What to answer? Admit that she was afraid he would make love to her again? Afraid he wouldn't? Riley said nothing; whatever she did say now would be wrong.

But Freyn wasn't to be denied. Striding back into the cottage, he left her standing at the door, but his voice was a whip.

'Well? Are you afraid I'm going to molest you or something? If so, I can assure you that you're perfectly safe, because rape isn't one of my specialities, nor is molesting young women, no matter how much they provoke me.'

She didn't reply, couldn't reply. Instead she leaned against the doorframe, her shoulders hunched beneath the sarcasm in his voice.

'Or are you afraid I won't fancy you at all?'

And now his voice was close against her ear; she could feel the warmth of his breath, and yet she hadn't heard him move.

The pungent scent of his aftershave touched her as

lightly as the fingers that brushed back the hair from her nape, but not as lightly as the lips that followed. And not nearly as light as the mist that captured her vision when those lips touched her.

Riley's mind told her to flee. Her body screamed at her to turn round, to meet his lips with her own. So she stood in total confusion, unable to do anything.

Then he was gone, as silently as he had arrived, and his voice came to her next from somewhere within the room.

'I'm going to have more coffee. Do you want some or not?'

The voice was cold, distant. So much so that she thought she must have imagined his gentle kiss. But she hadn't; Riley knew she hadn't.

'No, thank you,' she managed to reply, then straightened her shoulders and stood ramrod straight in the doorway, still gazing outward.

It took only another moment to regain her composure, whereupon she turned and walked calmly back to her seat. When Freyn sat down, a fresh cup of coffee nestled in his strong hands, she was able to meet his gaze without much trouble at all.

'What, specifically, did you want to discuss?' she asked in the most businesslike voice possible.

'What needs talking about the most urgently?'

'Nothing is all that urgent.'

'That,' he said, 'depends on your viewpoint. Surely there are aspects of your long-range plan that demand fairly immediate attention.'

'Only if you know a truly reliable wood hawker who really knows what he's about.'

'Don't you?'

'No, I'm afraid I don't. I could ask around, of course, but . . .'

'But since I have to make the ultimate decisions I'd

have to handle the hiring, I suppose. What's the logic behind it?'

'There's a great deal of timber here that's useless from a sawlog point of view. Over-mature, crooked, generally good for nothing but pulp, sleepers or firewood. And right now there's not much of a pulp market.'

'All of this useless timber, I presume, is taking up valuable growing space and nutrients from the trees with good potential.'

'That's generally it.'

'And I suppose it's in your way?'

'Only occasionally. That isn't really a problem.'

Freyn drained the cup, then without speaking he picked up both cups and stalked across the room to rinse them at the kitchen sink. Riley watched the dexterity with which he did the small washing up, noting how neat he was. Almost as if his aunt was still alive, might return to her kitchen at almost any moment and expect to find everything exactly in place as she had left it.

'How much supervision would that require on your part?'

He flung the question over his shoulder and didn't turn round to collect her answer.

'It would depend on who was involved. If my father was still alive he might know somebody. Mackie might. One of the problems is that good, straight young trees can be cut into sleepers as easily or more easily than crooked, big trees. There's always the temptation to——'

'You used to cut sleepers, didn't you?'

The interruption wasn't rude; it was simply that he had been thinking ahead of her answers, she thought.

'As I said, there's always the temptation.'

'But you don't always succumb to temptation, do you?'

Riley didn't answer. He was, she realised, deliberately baiting her. Had, perhaps, even steered the conversation along those lines just to give himself the chance.

Freyn didn't seem to care if she replied or not. It was as if he was determined to freeze her out of the picture.

'If we leave now, we'll catch Mackie before he's unloaded,' he said, folding the tea-towel neatly and then stooping to pick up the briefcase Riley hadn't even noticed beside his chair.

Lights off and the door locked behind them, Freyn stalked to his vehicle and thrust the briefcase into the back seat, not bothering to open the passenger door for Riley. For her part, she hardly noticed the lapse. Such courtesies weren't anything she had ever become accustomed to, doing a man's job in a man's world.

He drove skilfully, swiftly and silently on the return journey to the mill, and, upon arrival, Riley would have disembarked with similar silence had he given her the chance. But, 'We'll have a word with Julius Gunn,' he said just as the car halted. 'He may know of somebody who'll fit your criteria.'

Riley couldn't help the immediate flashback to her good days of working with Bill Gunn, but of course those days were over and had been for some time. And, in retrospect, she found herself wondering if they'd really been as good as memory recalled. Certainly they'd been pleasant, but compared to her reactions to Freyn Devereux at best, young Bill was, well, just that. Young.

And when they walked into Julius' office to find Bill there as well, she was immediately struck anew by the inherent differences between the men. Mackie's comment about Bill not being half the man his father was came immediately to mind. Freyn and Julius were a matched pair despite the difference in their ages, but Bill didn't seem to fit at all. Julius had a work-weary face that showed the scars of a hard, rough upbringing.

Freyn's rugged but handsome features held none of the scars, but still revealed the intense character beneath. Bill, who wasn't that much younger, looked somehow unfinished, not wholly formed as a person.

The comparison was something of a revelation.

CHAPTER FIVE

'YOU must be mad!'

Riley spoke the words into the telephone, then held the receiver from her, staring at it as if the thing had somehow come alive beneath her fingers.

'Not at all.'

The words emerged as if from a great distance, then strengthened as she returned the instrument to her ear.

'It's a perfectly legitimate conference, as you know very well, and there is every reason for both of us to attend,' Freyn's voice continued. 'Therefore, we shall; it's as simple as that.'

'Maybe simple to you, but certainly not to me,' Riley retorted in a bitter, angry voice. The nerve of this man! Did he really expect that she would obey him like some sort of slave? Or mistress?

'Look, Riley. Don't you think it's time you stopped being totally paranoid? I'm not asking you away for a wicked weekend, no matter what you may think. This is a very important conference on the taxation aspects related to private forestry. It's probably more important that *you* attend it than that I do.'

'And of course that explains why you give me two days' notice and expect me to just drop everything so that I can go with you?'

'I have been trying for three weeks to arrange it,' he said flatly. 'It wasn't until this morning that I had all the details confirmed.'

Which might have been true enough, Riley realised. Having only just got started in private forestry, Freyn probably wouldn't have had involvement with the forest development institute which was sponsoring the conference, or the state's private forestry council.

But if he *had* been trying for three weeks to become involved in the conference, why hadn't he said anything? She hadn't so much as seen him since their brief discussion with Julius and Bill Gunn almost a fortnight before, a discussion at which she might as well not have existed.

'Riley?'

And that was another thing, she thought. The use of her Christian name—something he had never done before tonight.

'Riley? Damn it, woman, have you hung up or what?'

'I'm still here,' she said in a voice that was flat despite the churning of emotion within her.

'Well, just see you're still there when I come to pick you up. Friday morning at six, sharp. Okay?'

He just ignored her protests as if they didn't exist! Clearly he had made up his mind she would attend the conference with him and that was that.

'Look,' she pleaded, 'I can't go with you. I . . . I . . .'

'Haven't got anything to wear, I suppose,' he chuckled, shooting down that argument before it even got off the ground. 'So, take tomorrow off and go shopping. I'll give you an advance if you need it. In fact, why not meet me for lunch, and I'll come with you.'

Riley's brain began to spin. How could he do this to her? He just always seemed to be one step ahead. And to think of going shopping with him *there* . . . Oh, no!

'I think I'd prefer to shop on my own,' she hurriedly replied, then gasped as she realised that by that statement she had as much as *agreed* to accompany him to the three-day conference in Launceston. At the Country Club Casino!

'You'll still need to eat. So let's agree to meet at Beards. It's central and the food's magnificent. Unless of course you'd prefer Wrest Point, just to give you a taste of what's in store for the weekend?'

Riley bit back the reply that was prompted by the decidedly wicked tone in his voice.

'Beards will do nicely,' she finally managed to say. 'About noon, I should imagine, although I may be a little late.'

She might be more than a little late, she thought, after he replied with a grin she could almost *see*. She might be three or four days late, just to put that arrogant man in his place.

'I'll look forward to it,' he said, as if butter wouldn't melt in his mouth. So gentle, so innocent, so filled with suggestive innuendo!

Or was that just her own interpretation?

She was no closer to knowing the answer to that when she approached the restaurant at ten past twelve the next day, having already circumnavigated the block three times just to force herself to be late.

It went against her grain, and yet she had been annoyed with herself at discovering on her initial arrival that she was actually a few minutes early. It was, she had already decided, all Freyn's fault. Riley had always been punctual, so why did this man have the ability to make her change so dramatically? She wasn't spiteful or vengeful, yet he seemed to bring out the very worst in her.

She thought for a moment of slipping into the Shamrock Hotel, over the road, where she could sip on a glass of white wine and spin away perhaps fifteen more minutes, then decided against it.

'Much as I need a drink,' she muttered, brushing some imaginary lint from her skirt before shoving open the door of Beards and stepping cautiously inside.

Almost at once, she knew she had made some horrible mistake. She ought to have chosen Wrest

Point, because Beards was a cosy, comfortable, *intimate* place. Exactly the place Freyn Devereux would take his women for lunch, or dinner, or whatever, she found herself thinking as the bearded proprietor approached with a welcoming smile.

It was no consolation at all to find him saying, 'Miss Jones? Mr Devereux will be delayed, I'm afraid. Please come and be seated; I'll bring you a drink.'

All that walking round the block for nothing, Riley thought with a wry grin, and in a token gesture to her tired feet, ordered a Piña Colada.

She devoted herself to wondering how the proprietor had recognised her, and whether Freyn's own lateness was as deliberately phony as had been her own.

What a hoot, she thought, if she had slipped into the Shamrock for a delaying drink, only to find him doing the same!

Five minutes later, she was on her second cocktail and surveying the extensive blackboard menu with tummy-growling interest. It was, she decided, quite innovative. Several of the dishes were distinctly tempting, and if Freyn didn't arrive soon, she would be trying them alone.

'Either that or have one more drink and be carried out of here,' she chuckled to herself. Then the chuckle died as a too-familiar figure approached from the doorway.

Riley suddenly felt terribly gauche in her simple dark skirt and white blouse. Freyn looked so—formal—in his superbly-cut business suit. It seemed to declare his masculinity, his successfulness, his quality.

And when he took her hand and bent over it, as if to proffer a kiss, Riley felt as if the entire restaurant was watching. It was somewhat disappointing when he merely brushed her knuckles with his lips, then glanced down towards her feet and raised one eyebrow.

'Shopping not too successful, I take it,' he said with a wry quirk of his lips. He sat down opposite her without waiting for a reply.

'I . . . well . . .'

She hesitated, unsure whether to lie and say her packages were in the truck, or admit she simply hadn't found anything—at *her* price—that seemed suitable for the weekend ahead.

Especially not, she thought, for whatever formal occasions might arise.

Riley's need for formal wear during the past few years had been very little different than it was before she started university—virtually non-existent.

But now, she knew instinctively what she liked, what would look excellent on her slim but curvaceous figure. However, she lacked, along with the simple matter of enough money, the knowledge of how to value such clothing, how to know what was a good buy and what wasn't.

Ridiculous, she had thought several times that morning, that she knew the best bargains in Hobart concerning blue jeans, work-shirts and logger's boots, but couldn't make a sensible selection of an evening gown to save her soul.

She had finished her morning's expedition in a state of mild confusion, now made worse by the fact that the blackboard menu in the restaurant contained a variety of goodies she wasn't even sure she could identify.

And, worse luck, Freyn Devereux seemed to have understood her dilemma.

'Shall I order for us both?' he asked, and at her nod and agreement that she was, indeed, quite hungry, he ordered game soup to start, followed by individual Beef Wellingtons for both of them.

The soup was tangy, tasty, and quite unlike anything she had ever tasted. So was the wine Freyn ordered, and

which Riley took sparingly in view of the drinks she had
already had. The main course was simply superb, and
when she had finished there was no room for dessert
and barely space for coffee.

Until Freyn's blonde entered the restaurant, homed
in on their table like a bee to honey, and rushed over
with a cry of delight. Then Riley's stomach suddenly felt
totally empty.

'Freyn ... darling! You didn't tell me you were
lunching here today.'

He greeted the woman without so much as trying to
avoid her long, possessive kiss, while Riley sat like a
frog on a log and wondered if the blonde truly thought of
herself as his keeper, or if she was merely making a
quite unnecessary point of staking her claim.

'Riley Jones, Clarice Downs.' Freyn might have
noticed the icy air between the two women; he kept the
introduction decidedly brief. But at least, Riley thought,
he didn't ask the blonde to join them.

Not that it made any difference. The exquisite
Clarice had only to glance imperiously around to have
an extra chair brought for her.

'I'll just join you for coffee,' she said with a sideways
glance at Riley. 'My party isn't here yet, and you know
they'll be late as always.'

Riley said nothing, although something inside her
writhed in torment, demanding to be allowed to make
some form of objection. How dared this blonde
bombshell invade her day, rain all over her parade?
And worse, do it so very deliberately.

The woman's attitude when she enquired into Riley's
circumstances was totally condescending, and became
even worse when Freyn answered, describing Riley too
accurately as his 'logging contractor'.

'How very ... interesting,' Clarice replied with a
wide-eyed glance that narrowed once it had swivelled

beyond Freyn's vision to confront Riley directly. Then
the eyes looked as if the blonde had suddenly been
confronted by a garden slug, or some other creepy-
crawly.

Riley replied with a blank stare.

'And tell me, dear. Do you actually go out and cut
down trees, and—well—whatever?' Clarice asked. The
manner was still condescending, so much so that Riley's
temper slipped just a trifle.

'Mostly whatever,' she replied, and cast what she
hoped was a knowing, suggestive glance in Freyn's
direction.

Did she only imagine the sudden twinkle in his eyes
when Clarice's eyes flashed ice? Riley herself took
immense delight in the success of the quick-thought
strategy, though she doubted she could hold her own for
long if Clarice decided to turn this brief skirmish into
full-scale war.

She quickly realised that Freyn, if no one else, was
quite enjoying the exchange. And, typical of the stirrer
that she knew him to be, he threw fuel on the fire by
blandly announcing his plans to take Riley up north to
the convention that weekend.

'We're just off to do a bit of last-minute shopping
when we've finished here,' he said with aplomb, and
Riley wished she could have laughed aloud at the
expression of absolute fury that flashed through
Clarice's eyes. Fortunately, any further confrontation—
with Clarice, at least—was spared by the arrival of her
party and the need for her to go and join them. But
confrontation had been implied, and Riley wasn't
letting it go that easily.

'How dare you?' she accused Freyn once the blonde
had sauntered to the far side of the restaurant and was
safely out of earshot.

'What *do* you mean?' he replied with a laugh that

made the question irrelevant. He knew very well what she meant, and he had enjoyed every stirring instant of it.

But Riley was unable to stop herself. Where Clarice had merely made her defensive and angry, Freyn made her absolutely furious.

'I mean that I don't enjoy being used, and furthermore that you can damned well go to your precious conference without me,' she proclaimed in a soft but icy voice.

'If I ever decide to *use* you, you'll know it,' he replied quietly. 'Now stop being defensive and let's go and see to that shopping, shall we?'

'I am quite capable of shopping by myself,' declared Riley sternly. 'And now, I don't need to, anyway.'

'You do unless you want to spend until Monday with only the clothes you're wearing,' he replied. 'Because you're coming with me to Launceston, whether you believe it or not.'

'Like hell I am!'

'Heaven or hell. It's all the same to me.'

And he rose lithely to his feet, depositing sufficient money on the table to cover the bill and more.

When Riley didn't get up to join him, he stood and looked down at her for an instant, then said, 'Come along, darling,' in a voice just loud enough to be heard at the adjoining tables.

'Touch me and I'll make a scene!' Riley whispered, her eyes wide with the almost certain knowledge that the threat would avail her very little indeed.

'Not as big as the one I'll make, carrying you out over my shoulder.'

He wouldn't dare! Or would he? One look into those expressive hazel eyes gave her the answer.

'Beast!' she hissed as she quickly arose and preceded him toward the door. But once out on the street, he took her arm with a smile as if he hadn't even heard.

Their shopping together was both a nightmare and an experience of astonishing intimacy and pleasure.

Riley found it frightening and embarrassing, at first. Freyn seemed to just take charge, and the fact that shop assistants obviously accepted his authority—meanwhile somehow assuming she was his fiancée, girlfriend, or whatever, and being obviously jealous!—did nothing to ease Riley's feelings.

But where she, personally, was concerned, he did no pushing, used no authoritarian tactics. He did, on the other hand, show no shyness about expressing his opinions. When she flatly rejected one dress he had liked, he grinned so hugely that it took her an instant to realise he had only been testing her, that he disliked the dress as much as she had.

The biggest problem was prices. He directed her to shops where quality was impressive and obvious, but the prices were, to her inexperienced eye, shocking. Worse, they were inevitably beyond her budget, but when she attempted to be firm on that score, his authoritarian attitudes came to the fore.

'Better than wasting money on rubbish,' he declared.

'Spending money I haven't got is worse than a waste,' she replied firmly in a whisper, sure the shop assistants could hear her.

'Well, you could let *me* spend it,' he replied with a grin that fairly shouted how likely a suggestion he knew that to be! 'Or just take the advance I offered you; surely there's nothing wrong with that.'

Riley sighed. At least he hadn't expected her to take his other suggestion seriously. But couldn't he realise that she needed to pay off logging equipment, not spend money she didn't have on clothes she didn't need?

But when she insisted on that ideal, he merely scoffed.

'You're a woman, and a lovely one to boot. Stop trying to bury your charms in the sawdust heap. Besides, how do you know you don't need them? Maybe they'll be called upon more often than you'd think.'

'Why don't you just take Clarice Downs to Launceston with you, and let me go back to my work?' Riley whispered in reply. But it was a waste of time arguing with Freyn Devereux.

'If that's what I wanted, it's what I'd have done.'

'And if I wanted to spend a fortune on clothes, I'd have done it without all this!' she replied after rejecting the fifth offering in a row from a slightly harassed young saleswoman. The girl, seemingly overwhelmed by Freyn, kept returning with dresses that grew more unsuitable for Riley even as their prices crept upwards.

'We'll try one last place,' he said with a frown, and Riley wondered if he was—finally—getting so bored with all this he'd leave her alone.

But it was not to be. The final shop proved to be her total downfall . . . or Devereux's revenge.

The very first garment brought for her assessment was a three-piece outfit in ivory-coloured, super-lightweight wool, with a skirt, a soft, long-lined, double-breasted jacket, and lean-cut pants. For evening the saleswoman brought out a backless halter-neck dress in a smoky blue raw silk. It was vividly daring, even when viewed from the front. Riley fell in love with the suit, but the halter-neck was definitely too adventurous!

Her objections might have been smoke.

'Perfect,' declared Freyn and indicated to the shop's manageress that he wanted to see more.

He didn't even look at the price tag, much to Riley's horror. She had, and was in a mild state of shock.

'I cannot wear that halter-neck,' she insisted in a whisper. 'I just couldn't!'

'Piffle. Of course you can. You'll look smashing in it.'

'Smashing? More like smashed. It's ... it's practically indecent!'

'Not if you have lovely shoulder-blades, as I'm sure you do.' And he was grinning, eyes laughing at her in wicked amusement, when the woman returned with a *second* outfit.

This was certainly less revealing—indeed, it was almost puritan by comparison. Exquisitely tailored in soft royal blue jersey, it was high-necked, slim-fitting and combined dress and over-jacket with very, very snug trousers.

Riley looked at the price tag and almost fainted, but her heart was already lost. And Freyn, the cunning devil, knew it!

'Right,' he said. 'Go and try them both on, and then we'll see about accessories.'

'Go and ... what?' Riley felt herself going all strange inside, as if her recent meal had turned into a thousand tiny balloons that were fighting now for flying room.

'Try them on. It would be appropriate, don't you think? Just to be certain they fit properly.'

She could only stare at him, wide-eyed. Of course she'd have to try them on, but here? Now? In front of him?

The saleswoman came to her rescue, leading Riley away to a set of changing rooms at the back of the shop, well distant from where Freyn waited.

'Start with this one,' the lady said, 'and I'll bring along a selection of blouses. Very light ones, I think. The weather's starting to warm up and of course you'll be indoors anyway.'

Riley's fingers shook as she peeled off her own outfit and tried on the first collection's skirt and jacket, then the trousers. All fitted perfectly.

The saleswoman returned with several blouses and the message that 'Your gentleman would like to see the dress, if you don't mind.'

'Then he'll have to wait,' Riley replied, knowing she could not model the halter-neck. Not here, not now.

'A wise decision. Better to keep a man on his toes,' smiled the saleswoman. 'All the better for effect when he does see it for the first time.'

Riley, calmed by the unexpected response, didn't bother to explain that there probably wouldn't *be* a first time; she just couldn't imagine herself wearing anything quite that revealing in public, and especially not for Freyn.

She tried on the blue outfit, which also fitted as if it had been made for her, then switched back to her street clothes, chose three of the blouses without a thought to the cost, and returned to where Freyn waited.

'Modest, I see,' he remarked in a low voice and with a characteristic lift of one dark eyebrow. Riley realised then that he hadn't truly expected her to model the dress; he had just been testing her in some strange manner known only to him.

'I was advised to save it for the right time and place,' she replied with what she hoped was a mysterious and haughty attitude.

It gained her only a momentary advantage, however, because moments later the parcels—and the bill— arrived. The amount rendered her truly speechless.

Freyn, typically, never so much as blinked. He handed over the amount, in cash, with a smile and a thank you to the well-contented sales lady, then gave Riley his arm and escorted her from the shop.

'What about accessories?' he asked.

'I think we'll start with a bankruptcy notice, just for starters,' she replied, after taking several deep breaths. It had all seemed quite unreal until they stepped into the warm afternoon sunlight. 'God, I must have been mad to let you talk me into spending that much money. I'll be working the rest of the winter just to pay *you* off, never mind my commitment to the bank.'

'You worry too much about money,' he replied as if it were totally unimportant.

'Yes, it comes from never having any,' she retorted, half inclined to snatch the parcels from his hands and rush back to return them. 'But then I suppose I shouldn't expect you to understand that . . .'

'I've done my share of going without,' he replied. 'And I'd do it again if I had to, without complaint. This time, you don't have to do without, so stop crying poor.'

'I'm not crying poor; I *am* poor. And I'll be a good sight poorer by the time I've repaid you!'

'But at least you'll look half decent while you're at it,' he replied with a grin.

'Half decent? Listen, mate. For what I've—you've—just spent, I'd better look a lot better than half decent. Anything less than fantastic and I've been cheated.'

'Oh, I don't think there's much chance of that,' Freyn replied. 'Considering I've seen you looking fantastic in your mechanic's outfit.'

Riley stopped dead in her tracks, all ready to throw the packages in his face. Then she realised, almost too late, that he wasn't laughing at her, that he had actually paid her a compliment.

'Thank you, I think,' she managed to say, then found herself continuing, 'although that doesn't say much for your taste.'

He merely grinned.

'There's nothing wrong with my taste. Or yours, for that matter; you've got a good eye for the types of clothes that suit you best.'

'It wasn't so good this morning,' she admitted ruefully. 'But then I didn't have the benefit of your experience and advice.'

'That,' Freyn advised with a half-frown, 'was very

close to being catty.'

'I suppose it was,' Riley admitted. 'But it wasn't meant to be, not really. In fact, I suppose I might as well confess that shopping with you was far less of an ordeal than I expected it to be.'

'You expected me to browbeat you into buying something you didn't like, I suppose?'

'Something like that.' Riley had to be vague, not wanting to admit that she didn't know exactly what she had expected, except for the knowledge that it wasn't what she'd got.

'Or was it that I didn't insist on you modelling everything? I thought about that, you know?'

'I'm sure you did. And I'm sure also that it's an area where you've had plenty of experience,' Riley replied.

He didn't even try to deny it.

'Only when I'm paying the bills. And of course you couldn't allow that.' It wasn't quite a question, but there was an enquiring lilt to his voice that seemed to demand an answer.

'It was bad enough having you advance me the money, thank you very much,' said Riley. 'Not to mention lunch, for which I also thank you. But to have you buying me clothes would be—well, let's just say the price of that would be more than I could afford.'

He shook his head in silent mirth, oblivious to the people who passed them on the footpath.

'What a strangely independent woman you are, Riley Jones. You walk around in the bush doing a man's job and taking insane financial risks, but with anything personal you're the soul of caution.'

'If I handled personal affairs like a man, you'd be accusing me of being too forward,' she replied stoutly. 'I can just imagine your reaction if *I* invited *you* away for a weekend conference.'

'This is a perfectly legitimate business affair,' said

Freyn, voice soft against the rush of traffic around them. 'And you can't imagine my reaction; not without putting your theory to the test. Which is something, dear girl, you're not brave enough to try.'

Too right! But she wouldn't give him the satisfaction of admitting it.

'You never know; I might surprise you one day,' she countered saucily, although she found it impossible to meet his gaze as she spoke.

'I'll look forward to it,' he replied, voice alive with that musical laughter she had come to expect whenever he had the upper hand and damned well knew it.

Riley still wasn't meeting his eyes, and it was something of a surprise when lean fingers cupped her chin, forcing her to lift her eyes.

'You wouldn't want to start by suggesting we leave a day early?' he said. 'We could go via Coles Bay, if you like.'

Even as her lips parted in a gasp of outrage, his mouth descended with inescapable certainty. Her outburst was destroyed in the softness of a kiss that lasted only an instant, yet seemed to go on for ever as he chained her with his eyes, with the touch of his fingers, of his mouth.

When he released her, Riley was torn between rioting feelings of anger, embarrassment and a strange regret that the kiss had ended.

'That was . . .' She floundered for words, her mind whirling in confusion.

'Despicable? Or should we try something more vivid, like *scandalous*? Or maybe *insulting*?' He was laughing at her, openly. 'Better yet, let's try something entirely different, like *very pleasant*.'

Riley could have cheerfully kicked him, but she felt— true or not—that everybody on the street was already staring at them.

'I've got a much better idea,' she replied with false

brightness, speaking through clenched teeth. 'Let's just settle for goodbye!'

'We can't.' His voice was awash with pretended sorrow, his eyes still sparkling as he relished her discomfort.

'Maybe *you* can't; I certainly can!'

'Only to say hello again on Friday morning, which means you should be saying *au revoir*; it's much more appropriate, after all.'

'You know where you can put your semantics,' Riley told him. '*And* your wretched conference with them.'

Freyn merely shook his head. 'I don't know what it is about you,' he remarked. 'You enjoyed being kissed a moment ago, but you won't admit that even to yourself. You enjoy my company, at least some of the time, but you won't admit that either, especially to me. If I didn't know better, I'd think you didn't like me at all.'

'If you didn't spend so much time being an egotistical brute you'd understand it perfectly,' Riley parried. 'Now, if you don't mind, I'm sick of this game and I want to go home.'

'Pity. The afternoon's just about shot anyway; I was going to suggest we finish our shopping and start thinking about a drink before dinner.'

He made the comment with one eyebrow raised in a gesture that totally ignored her anger, her embarrassment, her entire attitude.

'I don't believe this!' she said, voice shaking from sheer incredulity. 'Are you really so obtuse that you can't get it through your head that I'm angry, that I don't *want* to finish *our* shopping, that all I want to do is remove myself from your annoying company? You must be as thick as two short planks!'

'Why? You're not angry with me. You're angry with yourself because you're feeling trapped. And the only reason you want to be shot of me is because I make you feel uncertain of your feelings. You didn't really mind being kissed, Riley. You just minded not being asked first.'

'Oh, for the love of . . . Look, will you please spare me the psychoanalysis? I don't need you to tell me who I'm angry at and why.'

'You just can't stand it when you're not totally in control, can you?'

Riley gritted her teeth, fighting to maintain sanity in the face of this insufferable assault.

'And I suppose you can?' she asked then, her voice taut with venom.

'I don't know; I've never been in that situation,' Freyn replied with maddening ease. 'Now what'll it be—a drink before we finish shopping, or finish first and then have a drink?'

'How would it be if you go for your drink, and I'll finish my shopping . . . alone!'

He smiled, the mischievous, bright-eyed smile of a small boy successful in conspiracy. 'What a splendid compromise. Okay, I'll meet you in the lounge bar at Maloney's just before six,' he said. 'They've got a chef there who does proper, American-style spare ribs and wondrous things with chicken wings and stuff.'

Riley didn't answer, didn't so much as nod. But he took her silence for acceptance, so it seemed, and a moment later she saw the back of him, striding away from her with his usual maddening confidence.

Finishing the shopping was an anticlimax; getting back to the Centrepoint car park before it closed was a last minute panic. But it was after that when things started to get really tricky.

Riley had barely been able to believe her luck when Freyn took his leave, insisting on her promise to meet him later. And having made no promises, she certainly had no intention of accepting his suggestion.

'I have had enough of you, Mr Freyn Devereux, to last me for the rest of my life,' she muttered to herself as she negotiated the ramps of Centrepoint. The passenger side of the little truck was filled to overflowing with her day's purchases.

'All I really want is to go home,' she continued.

However, to get home she would pass within spitting distance of Maloney's, and by the time she had got that far, Riley knew she might as well look for a parking spot and face the evening ahead as best she could. She could fight Freyn Devereux in anger, but she couldn't be deliberately rude, not like this, in cold blood.

Damn him! He had known her eventual reaction even before she had, because he could play upon her emotions, her character, her personal attitudes as if they were part of some living musical instrument for which he could alter the score at will.

Parking the truck, she marched determinedly through the swinging doors into Maloney's, her eyes searching out Freyn even as her lips formed their defence for being so late.

Both gestures were wasted. He wasn't there, didn't arrive during the next hour—in which hunger drove her to test his recommended spare ribs and approve them heartily in spite of herself—and hadn't arrived when she finally left in a towering rage after still another hour.

Worse, he didn't arrive or telephone with any explanation the following day. Or send flowers. Or . . .

CHAPTER SIX

FRIDAY morning's departure was so chilly they might have been leaving from the Antarctic.

Freyn arrived punctually at six, to find Riley—equally punctual despite severe misgivings—waiting on the doorstep.

With only the briefest of nods, he handed her into the passenger seat, then loaded her baggage and returned to his own place behind the wheel.

'Last chance to remember whatever it is that you're sure to have forgotten.' he commented with a smile that brought him only a frozen nod in reply.

Riley didn't want humour, and certainly not humour as forced as that. What she did want, and wasn't game to insist on, was some explanation.

Freyn didn't appear to notice her silent appeals.

He drove north in silence, up through Campania, then Colebrook, and finally turned on to the Midland Highway just past Jericho. If he sensed Riley's growing tension, the frustration that crept up to swell in her throat, he didn't show it. Worse, he didn't show any sign of suffering such problems himself.

It was *he* who had arranged to meet her at Maloney's; *he* who had made that arrangement knowing she wouldn't want to keep the date but would be forced to by her own conscience, and *he* who hadn't even bothered to show up!

Riley hadn't been able to believe her ears when she had finally, having finished the spare ribs, summoned up the nerve to ask the barmaid if Freyn Devereux was, by chance, somewhere else in the establishment. After

114

all, she had been somewhat later than their so-called agreement. Perhaps he had been unable to wait, or had shifted to the dining room.

But the barmaid's reply, accompanied by a sort of dreamy look at the mention of the name, killed that.

'Freyn Devereux? No, love, haven't seen him for days,' was the reply, including the unspoken guarantee that if Freyn had been in, this barmaid would have remembered.

The brute! Riley found her thoughts screaming despite the calming effect of the excellent meal. He hadn't even bothered to keep the appointment he, himself, had made! It wasn't that she had been late; he just hadn't bothered to show up. Unbelievable!

The fact that she had been planning exactly the same thing only poured fuel on the fires of her anger. How dare he?

They were just through St Peter's Pass, swinging down towards the Antill Ponds rest area with its stunning examples of topiary, when Riley finally exploded.

'Aren't you going to say *anything* about Wednesday night?' She cried out so unexpectedly, her voice so shrill with pent-up frustration, that he almost swerved off the highway.

'What do you want me to say?'

His voice was calm, reasonable, infuriating.

'Well, an apology would be a nice start.'

'I suppose so. All right—I apologise.'

Riley couldn't believe it. Was this all there was to it? A simple, even humble apology? No argument, no excuses, no room for her to vent the frustration that had cost her two nights' sleep and a day of wasted emotional turmoil?

'Not enough!' She almost screamed it.

'What isn't?'

Ah, she thought, now we're getting somewhere. Or had she imagined that slight tone of irritation in his voice?

'Do you know how long I waited for you? Alone! Hungry! In a strange bar.'

The edges of his mouth started to twitch, but before he did anything else, he hurriedly turned on his indicator and swung the big car into the rest area, sliding to a hasty stop on the gravel.

Then the twitching became a definite chuckle and that magnified in an instant to become an explosion of scarce-controlled laughter. His eyes streamed with tears as he shook his head, one fist pounding at the steering wheel as he fought for control.

Then Riley, too, exploded. Only her outburst wasn't laughter; it was a volcano of white anger, shimmering rage.

'Damn you. It's not funny. It isn't!'

To no avail. He only laughed the harder, at first. But finally her rage managed to tower over his sense of humour, to strangle it into some form of submission. Strong hands reached out to capture her flailing fists, and she heard his voice like a great distant thunderstorm.

'Settle down. Steady, for God's sake.'

'It's ... it's not funny,' she hiccuped in a final demand for attention.

Then she did steady, did settle down, at least enough to see half clearly the still twitching expanse of his mouth before he spoke.

'I gather you're trying to tell me I outsmarted myself the other night? That you actually did keep our dinner date at Maloney's?'

'Which *you* didn't.' And she put every scathing implication she could into those three words, every bit of scorn and anger she had been feeling since she had known the certainty of having been stood up.

'Well ...!' He was shaking his head as if in astonishment, but he hadn't released her wrists, and he was looking into her eyes with a most quizzical expression.

Before she could move, he leaned forward to kiss her, ever so lightly and quickly, on the forehead.

'Well, I'm damned,' he said, shaking his head again. ' You are just full of surprises, young Riley. And I do indeed apologise, thrice over. Five times over, in fact, because I believe that's the first time I've *ever* stood a girl up.'

He continued to stare into her eyes, his own glance softening as laughter gave way to something else.

'And of course it had to be you,' he said in a voice that also was subtly changed, softened. 'You did keep our dinner date. I'd never have imagined it! When I left you on the street, I wasn't sure you'd even be on deck this morning, and I would have sworn you were going to stand *me* up on Wednesday night.'

'Thank you so much for the vote of confidence,' Riley replied with dripping scorn. She fought with the conscience that demanded she admit, at least, to having been almost an hour late for that dinner engagement.

Fatal mistake. He either read her mind or guessed—too correctly for comfort.

'You were a fair bit late, though?'

It wasn't totally a question.

'A little.' She would admit to no more.

'At least half an hour. Probably more like an hour.'

Now she saw the return of his old self. The total confidence, the sheer masculine power seemed to flow like a tide of energy through his body. She could feel it in the way his fingers gripped—still—at her wrists.

'How would you know? You weren't even there at all!' she cried. But it was too late. His instincts had been aroused, his suspicions were alive.

'I couldn't get a parking space anywhere near the place,' he said. 'So I did a fair bit of driving round the block, and your distinctive little truck wasn't there either.'

'Which proves what? Some of us, my dear Mr Devereux, aren't afraid of a bit of a walk. Or hadn't you considered that?'

'You were not there before six-thirty at the absolute earliest.'

'I . . .' She couldn't lie.

'And since you have to be out of Centrepoint by that time, logic tells me you were either deliberately late to Maloney's, or that you had a bit of a drive around while you thought about whether to stand *me* up or not. Deny it?'

Deny it? She would rather have drowned him in it.

'I got out of Centrepoint at the absolute last minute,' she countered futilely. 'Another ten seconds and they'd have locked me in for the night.'

She couldn't sustain the righteous indignation. He was too close to the truth and they both knew it. Now. But his next words were far from what she expected.

'Still, you did show up eventually. Which I didn't. So I apologise, sincerely I do. I shall try to make it up to you by providing a truly fantastic weekend.'

His lips descended again, only this time they searched for—and found—her own.

The kiss was, at first, so gentle as to seem almost tentative. But only at first. Freyn's lips held a world of experience beyond anything Riley could even imagine, and within seconds his mouth was tantalising her, teasing and touching and teasing some more until she began to react.

This was no brutal assault; rather it was a compelling, a drawing out of her very sexuality. Because of his grip on her wrists, locking both their arms between them, and because of their position within the vehicle, Riley should easily have been able to pull away.

But she didn't, and in fact she didn't even try.

As her lips parted to receive the soft warmth of his breath, the probing exploration of his tongue, her own breath grew short, and she could feel her breasts rising and falling against the warmth of his forearms. Then his fingers released her, and her arms lifted as if by magic to creep across his shoulders, pulling against the tense neck muscles in an involuntary attempt to draw him closer, to tighten their embrace.

Freyn's left arm had shifted to slide in behind her waist, and his right hand was busy assisting in the systematic plunder of her defences.

She felt his touch, feather-light at her throat, his fingers tracing the cord of muscle downward to the hollows above her breast-bone. An instant later, his lips followed, their path a trace of ice and fire that poured liquid-smooth through the opening of her shirt.

Then his lips returned to capture her mouth again, but his fingers remained to twitch open buttons, exposing the swell of her breasts to a more exquisite exploration.

Fitting with astonishing ease into the minute space between their bodies, her own fingers were on an exploration of their own, teasing open the buttons of his shirt to flicker through the dense mat of his chest hair.

Riley was beyond caution, beyond any sense of logic or morality. Even her customary fear of her own inexperience had dissipated in the storm of raw sensuality that melted her limbs, flooded her brain with a kaleidoscope of emotion. She heard his slight hiss of satisfaction with the touch of his fingers against warm, pliant, flesh; she took delight in his pleasure.

The mouth that continued to plunder her own did so

now with increased urgency, an urgency matched by the tide of wanting inside her. She wanted him. Wanted him now, here, totally.

Her own hand had strayed to his belt buckle, and now moved lower, searching independently of her consciousness, searching by orders from her inner sexuality. And searching with startling success.

Now she was conscious of the moan that escaped his lips; she was also conscious of the softer, more insistent moan that escaped her own.

And then both of them were conscious of a louder moan, a more insistent moan—the strident moan of the air-horn on a passing semi-trailer. It was like being dashed with icy water. And worse.

As they drew apart, eyes locked as if in an attempt to prolong their contact, Riley's mind returned to her, and she felt a flicker of fear at the naked, raw desire she saw in the hazel eyes only inches away. But that was nothing compared to the shudder of distaste at the publicness of their situation, at the immediate thought of what the truck-driver must have seen, or at least imagined.

Her fingers flew to straighten her clothing. Her eyes broke the bond between herself and Freyn, her conscience whipped at her, bringing a tide of scarlet from breast to throat.

She looked at him again, eyes wide as saucers, then widening further under the impetus of guilt. She turned and fumbled for the door handle, then stumbled from the car to flee with a shambling gait along the narrow footpath that led over a tiny bridge and then up to the washrooms.

Freyn's eyes followed. She felt them, hated them.

The flush of shame was gone by the time she reached the restroom. A stranger stared at her from the mirror, with enormous, slate-grey eyes in a face the colour of old snow. A stranger with a mind as confused as her own, with a body still trembling, still shivering from the ice in her belly.

She splashed water on to her face, shook her head as if that might somehow clear away the memories, and finally fought her way back to control with a long series of deep breaths.

But what now? Her every instinct was to flee, but there was nowhere to run. She had only her handbag with her; her jacket and luggage remained in Freyn's car.

And yet . . . could she face him? Did she even want to?

'I must,' she told the distraught figure in the mirror. She tried to mentally suppress the conscience that insisted on trying to share the blame for what had happened. She hadn't encouraged him! She hadn't done anything, hadn't said anything, hadn't even thought anything!

But she had felt it. From the instant of seeing him that morning, the maintenance of her anger had been a conscious thing, an exercise that required deliberate thought. She had dressed for Freyn, choosing the classic business suit, the tidy silken blouse, over the subtle attractiveness of stockings and garter-belt. From the instant of his arrival at her door, she had been aware of him, her nostrils alive to the scent of his aftershave, her eyes drinking in the line of his features, the roughness of his typically rumpled hair. There had been no fear when he had grabbed her wrists, only a sort of gladdening at the touch of his strong, masculine fingers. And no opposition—not a whit of it— from the instant of his first kiss to the embarrassing interruption that had ended their lovemaking. Riley had wanted it, and knew that Freyn realised that as thoroughly as she herself.

Worst of all was the simple truth. Until the rudeness of the interruption, until shame had been summoned by a horn—it had been so right!

Too right. It left her too vulnerable, now, too totally aware of her own responses, of Freyn's unquestionable desire. How could she possibly get through three days of being almost constantly in his company?

He made the decision easy for her, or at least as easy as it could be, when she returned finally to the car to find him sitting comfortably on one of the log barriers surrounding the parking area.

'I won't apologise this time,' he said, rising at her approach and meeting her eyes without revealing any hint of his own feelings, 'but I will—if you absolutely insist—turn round and take you home.'

'And if I don't?'

He grinned, shrugged. 'Well then, I guess it's on to the wilds of Launceston and whatever the weekend holds in store.'

'And does that include a promise to behave yourself?' Riley was astonished at her own forthrightness, at the calmness of her voice, the inward acceptance that nothing between her and Freyn Devereux could ever be the same again. But mostly at her sudden realisation that she no longer feared that.

'I will if you will.'

And he wasn't trying to shift the blame, or even to share it—she sensed that immediately. He was, in fact, putting the ball squarely in her court with a simple statement that should have sounded flippant but didn't.

Riley felt that she stood on the edge of a precipice, with faulty balance and nothing much to grab for support. Her mind spun back to the first really big tree she had ever felled, to the instant when she had gone too far to retreat, when the screaming of the saw was replaced by the visceral shudder as the giant began to topple. It had been a tiny moment of gut-wrenching terror and triumph that she would never wholly forget.

She shook her head, not in a negative gesture, but in that swift jerkiness of a decision made.

'I won't get breakfast if I go home, because the fridge is empty,' she said. 'And if I don't get breakfast pretty soon, I will be very, very cranky.'

'I know just the place,' Freyn replied, the words emerging on a deep exhalation that Riley's imagination thought just might have been a sigh of relief.

'Just the place' turned out to be another hour's drive away, a roadhouse in the highway junction town of Perth. Riley watched in quiet fascination as Freyn demolished one of the biggest T-bone steaks she had ever seen, quite ignoring the comparable assault she made on an omelette that rivalled the steak in size and thickness.

'We could have gone on to the casino, I suppose, and started our day with eggs Benedict,' Freyn mused about halfway through the steak.

'And I'd have chewed your arm off before you'd got fifty yards past this place,' Riley mumbled through a mouthful of her omelette.

It was astonishing how things between them had just . . . clicked into place once she had decided not to run for home and the safety of the past. True, nothing could ever be the same again. But it didn't matter, because their relationship had somehow grown, and in the growing it had improved. She wasn't sure what the weekend held in store, was even less certain of her reaction if he should try to make love to her again. But that didn't matter. She was going to enjoy herself come what may.

They had left the roadside rest area in silence, and driven in silence as far as Perth, but it was a comfortable silence, one in which Riley had been able to relax, to try and order her thoughts.

Yes, Freyn's lovemaking had carried her to new

heights, had awakened feelings and emotions and needs she hadn't even been aware existed. But he hadn't done it cruelly, hadn't taken unfair advantage.

And hadn't done it without her willing compliance!

Most important, she instinctively knew that unless she gave him the opportunity, unless she relaxed her guard, he wouldn't so much as lay a hand on her during their stay in Launceston. There was a comfort in that, and at the same time an emotion-heightening, almost dizzying sense of risk. Because she knew—and so did he—that part of her wanted him to make love to her, to fulfil the promise of his kisses, of his caresses. Her emotional future hung on a slender thread of luck, timing and precarious judgement. Freyn Devereux was far too experienced for her, and Riley knew the price of such experience would be—for her—immensely high.

But the price of having backed away, of having forced him to return her to the safety of her past, was also high, because it offered neither risk nor prize nor challenge.

And for Riley—today's Riley—that just wasn't quite enough. Not that she had any intention of falling into Freyn Devereux's bed, much less of falling into the emotional minefield her own senses had laid. But she could, and would, take her employer's largesse in the spirit with which it had been originally offered. She would wear her finery, pamper her ego, and guard her emotions as if from the devil himself.

As she finished her breakfast, wondering how she could ever be expected to eat another bite during the rest of the day ahead, she thrust into her mind the cool self-assurance of Freyn's blonde lover, remembering the icy chic, the poise, the veneer of haughty dignity. Riley Jones couldn't compete with Clarice Downs for loveliness, and she wouldn't try to compete in bed. But she could and would give the blonde a run for her money in providing Freyn with a companion of whom other men would be justifiably envious.

Riley Jones would be beautiful!

Such thoughts sustained her during the remainder of their journey, and by the time they arrived at the sprawling hotel-casino complex, she was reasonably relaxed about the weekend ahead.

The hotel-casino, at first glance, resembled a super-stretched colonial mansion. Constructed of cream-coloured brick, the windows and pillars and eaves all shining white, it provided a much subdued atmosphere when compared to the ultra-visible tower of Hobart's Wrest Point casino.

Inside, the country club look was maintained by a décor of greens and beiges, with widespread use of wood to give a sense of quiet luxury. Outside, the impression was enhanced by vast lawns and a beautifully designed man-made lake.

As they approached the registration desk, Riley suddenly felt horribly conspicuous. Freyn, typically, took charge of their registration, and although it was accomplished with no fuss at all, she felt as if everyone in the lobby was staring at her, speculating on her relationship with this tall, handsome man. For an instant, she half poised to flee, her own eyes darting quick glances at the dozens of people who seemed all to be just waiting for just such a move.

But then it was too late; Freyn had turned to take her arm, and was escorting her along the wide corridor leading to the accommodation section.

He said nothing, but stepped out so briskly she had almost to trot to keep up with him, and her earlier fears were somehow lost in the long trek to their rooms.

'I'll take care of our conference registrations,' he said, 'and then I've a few things to do in Launceston this afternoon. The first conference function is dinner tonight, so let's plan on me collecting you at six and we'll have a drink first.'

'Fine. I'm sure I can keep myself busy until then,' she replied. 'Actually, a nap wouldn't go astray, if you're sure there's nothing you want me to do.'

'Relax and enjoy yourself, that's all. And don't start your nap just for a bit, because I'll be sending somebody along with all the conference bumph as soon as I get it together. That way you'll have the chance to figure out what seminars you want to pass up in favour of more entertaining pursuits.'

'Such as?'

Her voice was wary, but he only grinned wickedly. 'How should I know?'

Then he was gone, leaving Riley in the unaccustomed luxury of a room that suddenly seemed strangely empty.

She spent the next ten minutes laying out her clothing, and had only just finished that when a knock on the door announced the arrival of her conference material. Sprawled across the bed, she spent half an hour going through the material, but found her attention span almost non-existent. None of the guest speakers were familiar to her, and most of the conference subjects—while significant—seemed more related to business management than to forestry itself.

'Still, it's all stuff I'll have to come to terms with in the long run,' she said, talking to herself aloud although unaware she was doing it. But it was slightly depressing to realise how very much she had still to learn about her chosen profession.

The disruptions of her morning had left her fidgety, restless. She tried to nap, couldn't and finally changed to her swimsuit and navigated her way to the indoor, heated pool. It was a blessing to have that facility entirely to herself, and she took full advantage. The afternoon passed in a repeated series of long, punishing swims and short, breathless rest periods. After the exercise, a nap came easily, and Riley wakened with only just enough time to prepare for the evening ahead.

The opening dinner would, because of the welcoming speeches and keynote address, be fairly lengthy, Freyn told her when he telephoned her room just before five.

'But there'll still be time for a dance or two if you're so minded, or a flutter at the tables.'

Riley wasn't about to be pinned down.

'Let's see how we feel when the time comes,' she replied, her mind half occupied with the decision about what to wear. Not that it was all that difficult. The ivory suit or the royal blue jersey, because the halter-neck was very definitely out!

In the end, she chose the jersey, thinking it would be the more sensible of the two outfits. If nothing else, it was the least revealing, which somehow seemed important.

Freyn, as she had come to expect, was prompt. His knock at her door caught her only just prepared, and she was mildly smug at not being tardy herself.

And, also as expected, he was resplendent in a dark dinner suit, shoes that gleamed like mirrors, and his face freshly shaven. The faint aura of his shaving lotion was like a tonic.

He stood in the doorway, eyes assessing her with a look that was neither over-bold nor challenging. He did, however, obviously like what he saw.

'Very nice indeed,' he said. 'And I won't say "I told you so" even though we both know I could. That outfit was made for you.'

'It wasn't the style I objected to, if you remember,' Riley smiled, determined to avoid any sort of conflict on this official start to their weekend.

'And what did you do with your day?' he asked as

they strolled down the long corridor, arm-in-arm. He had altered his pace to suit Riley's much shorter stride, and in her unaccustomed high heels, she was grateful for the extra support his arm gave her.

'Mostly swam.'

'That'd be right,' he said in a voice that expressed neither surprise nor disappointment.

'And what's that supposed to mean?'

He smiled warmly. 'Just that I wouldn't have expected you to launch yourself into an orgy of gambling, or take the restaurant by storm. Stop being so testy.'

'Well, I could hardly be expected to take any restaurant by storm after that enormous breakfast, or brunch, or whatever you want to call it,' she replied. 'And as to the rest, I can't afford to gamble and I'm *not* being testy.'

'Okay, but I warn you that *I* will be if there are too many before-dinner speeches.'

And to her astonishment, he lifted her hand to his lips and then bared his teeth in a ferocious grimace.

'So just be warned, because in that outfit you look eminently edible. Dessert, perhaps?'

'You just remember that I bite back,' she warned, her voice soft now as she realised there were other people about. Many other people. 'And please behave yourself! What will people think?'

'Who cares?'

'I do, for one. And you should.'

'I'm not in the habit of running my life to suit the whims of strangers.'

He said it with the quiet confidence she had come to expect. But when they entered the spacious conference room a moment later, and found their seats at a table filled with strangers, Freyn changed his tune.

His quiet assertiveness was exchanged for smiling

charm that within moments brought Riley glances of
envy from some of the other women at the table. And
they were married!

Glancing round, she saw virtually no one she
recognised, but quickly realised that whatever women
were present, they were with their husbands. It didn't
require a look at their ring fingers to confirm that; they
looked married.

'Do I?'

She wasn't aware of having whispered the question
aloud, until Freyn asked, 'Do you what?', leaving her to
fumble for an innocuous reply.

'Nothing. Just thinking out loud,' she managed. 'I
expect it's because, like you, I'm suddenly hungry.'

But she wasn't.

In fact, it was an effort to force down the quite
excellent meal that was provided in an extensive buffet
of hot and cold dishes. Riley's mind was numbed by her
own reaction to her own question, and thoughts of food
just couldn't keep their footing.

Did she look married?

It was a deliciously challenging thought, like standing
high on a cliff and looking down. She didn't *feel*
married, but there was certainly a sense of possessive-
ness created by the mildly envious glances from other
women.

And if she didn't look married to Freyn, then why the
jealous looks? Would a married woman feel envious just
because someone else was with a man she fancied?
Someone with no claim whatsoever, perhaps, but at
least a better chance of reaching him? It was thought-
provoking; certainly more so than the various speeches
that accompanied the meal. Riley heard them all, but
they went in one ear and out the other. She was far too
conscious of the tall man beside her, of the sound of his
voice, the movement of his strong, agile fingers through

the cutlery, the occasional touch of his knee against hers. Here he was a different person, somehow, from the man she had driven north with, the man who had so thoroughly insinuated himself into her own life-style.

This was his territory, the corporate world, the world of movers and shakers and boardroom pirates. Gradually, as her own situation came under better control, she was able to realise how thoroughly Freyn could draw out his neighbours at the table, sifting through their conversation, steering that conversation to give him every possible nugget of information.

And she realised that it wasn't a malicious or even deliberate manipulation. He was simply interested; therefore he listened, probed, listened some more.

And yet always, she knew, with an inherent awareness of herself, there beside him. It wasn't blatant, but there was some silent leash between them that kept him constantly aware of her own needs. When her wine glass was empty, he was there. When she needed butter, he passed it before she could ask. All this despite the fact he hardly spoke to her during what few opportunities there were.

Polite, charming, efficient, and . . . so aware!

Table conversation picked up again immediately the keynote speaker was finished, only now the atmosphere in the conference room seemed to take on a lighter, gayer note. Some people began to table-hop, greeting old and distant friends and picking up on old conversations, past meetings. It made little difference to Riley; she knew virtually no one in the room and was in any event content to just sit and people-watch.

Freyn seemed settled into a vigorous conversation with a man on his right, but it ended without warning the instant the band started to play.

'Our time, now, I think,' he said, turning to Riley with a smile and rising lightly to his feet. His fingers closed over hers with gentle insistence, his eyes made it more than clear that she had the full focus of his attention.

He danced divinely, more than compensating for her own shortcomings with his perfect rhythm, his masterful ability to plot a perfect course round the dance floor. Riley gave herself entirely to his direction, dancing better than she ever had in her life, and loving it.

The remainder of the evening flew past in a blur of colour and movement as she gave herself over to the sheer pleasure of it all. They danced, and danced some more, pausing only during the breaks, resting only when the band rested.

When the band finally shut down, Riley was despondent. She wanted it to go on for ever, but five minutes later she began to fade, and realised that her day full of exercise was starting to take its toll.

'Come on, Cinderella. I think it's time we got you tucked up in bed before you turn into a pumpkin,' Freyn said with a warm smile. Riley wanted to argue, wanted to suggest they go on to Regine's Disco, elsewhere in the complex, to continue this blissful existence in Freyn's arms. But she couldn't. Instead, she allowed herself to be guided back along the lengthy corridor, allowed him to take her key, open her door, and return the key to her with only a token kiss on the forehead.

'To bed, before you fall asleep right where you're standing,' he said in a voice that seemed hypnotic in the fuzziness of her mind.

'Don't want to sleep. Want to dance.'

His laugh was as gentle as his voice. 'You may want to dance, little one, but you *need* to sleep. Don't forget we have a long day ahead of us tomorrow.'

Riley would have argued more, but her eyes wouldn't focus properly and her legs, unaccountably, had turned to trembling, wobbly structures that couldn't possibly support her weight for much longer.

She swayed, steadied herself against the strong arm that captured her waist. She was lifted, guided across the room, placed in one of the large, soft armchairs.

Freyn strode back to shut the door, then over to turn down the bed covers. Riley watched, but didn't really comprehend.

Not, that was, until he returned to lift her to her feet and began to undress her!

She let out a squeal of dismay, but Freyn ignored it as he quickly slipped off the jacket of her outfit, then started removing the dress itself.

'Stop it!'

She pushed feebly at him, trying to steady herself on rubbery legs.

'Oh, stop fussing, unless you want to sleep in this gear and wrinkle it beyond salvation,' he replied grimly, and steadied her as he continued undoing the dress.

'I . . . I can do it myself,' she insisted, and swayed, would have fallen but for his grip.

'You're too tired to do anything for yourself,' he growled. 'Now stop being stupid. I'm not going to hurt you.'

'You are hurting me!'

'Don't be silly.'

He had the dress completely undone, now, and implacably began the process of wriggling Riley out of it.

It was too easy. He was too strong, too confident; and Riley was, indeed, too tired to argue. An instant later she was flat on her back on the bed, legs hanging over the edge, and he was expertly divesting her of the jersey trousers.

'Right. You can sleep in the rest,' he said, the huskiness of his voice matching the undisguised flash of desire in his eyes. Calmly he gathered her in his arms, spun once around the room, then thumped her on to the bed and whisked the covers over her.

'Good night,' he said.

He kissed her lightly on the lips, then turned away. He was halfway to the door when she thought she heard him say, 'And *I'll* get out of here before I do something really stupid.'

Or did he? She lay for a moment, debating that, watching the room slowly revolve. It was so restful, so incredibly soothing.

What had he said? She fought to retrieve the words, certain that they'd been important, certain that she must remember, that his parting comment was highly significant to her own confused feeling.

But before she could sort everything out, she tumbled into sleep, smiling.

CHAPTER SEVEN

IN the morning, Riley thought she would die. And wished she could!

In retrospect, it was easy to see her mistake; gulping down white wine to ease her thirst seemed fine while she was still dancing, but it was inevitable and savage in its revenge later. Her head throbbed, her stomach was filled with butterflies and her feet hurt, but the biggest damage was to her self-esteem.

What must Freyn Devereux think? 'The worst. Absolutely the worst,' she muttered, staring bleary-eyed into the mirror.

Habit had betrayed her with a dawn awakening, and she knew any return to sleep, however much needed, would be impossible.

Moving with great care, she gathered her clothes from the night before and put them away, then debated what to do next.

'Disappearing would be a great idea,' she said to the haggard reflection in the bathroom mirror as she gathered the strength to shower. If that had been a possible solution, Riley would have grabbed at it, but it wasn't. So she chose the next best thing—a swim.

'If nothing else, it'll clear my head,' she muttered, stalking through the silent corridors *en route* to the pool.

And she was right. The first few laps were agony, but as she deliberately forced her body back and forth through the water, she began to feel greatly better.

A rest, then ten more laps, and she would at least be fit enough for breakfast, she thought. As for facing the justified wrath of Freyn Devereux—well, she would worry about that on a full stomach.

She was almost at her door when a familiar voice from behind made her turn with alarm and surprise.

'Bill? What are you doing here?' she asked as Bill Gunn approached, his eyes bleak with anger.

'Well, I'm not here to make a fool of myself like you, that's for sure,' he replied grimly. and reached out to snatch the room key from her grasp.

'What are you talking about?' Riley gasped as he opened the door and thrust her inside.

'Your little performance last night, just for starters,' he snapped. 'Have you lost your mind Riley? Or are you so infatuated with Devereux that you don't care what people think?'

'And what am I supposed to have done last night that was so bad?' demanded Riley, her own anger rising now to match Bill's. 'Is there a law all of a sudden against dancing, having a good time?'

'And then taking Devereux back to your room for more good times? If there isn't, there should be,' he snarled. 'And don't bother to deny it; I've got eyes.'

Riley felt her stomach churn, the forgotten butterflies suddenly alive and flying again.

'I . . . we . . .'

'Don't bother trying to explain,' Bill sneered. And as he leaned towards her in anger she could smell the whisky on his breath.

It took an instant for her mind to register the fact; then she recoiled in a muddle of anger and shame and indignation. Bill Gunn was drunk, or next thing to it.

'I think you'd better go,' Riley said, suddenly conscious of the thin wrap that covered her bikini, indeed *too* conscious of how little the entire outfit concealed.

In Bill's bloodshot eyes she could see the mingling of anger with lust, the sullen, childish desire for revenge. It didn't need any imagination to visualise what form that revenge might take, given half a chance.

For the first time, Riley felt fear, and she stepped back, trying to put space between her and Bill. She had to fight to believe what was happening; this was Bill Gunn, whom she had grown up with. And yet, somehow, it wasn't.

This Bill Gunn was angry, frustrated, and Riley suddenly realised just how much she must have offended him with her constant rebuffs. Hell hath no fury, she thought, and would have giggled except she was too frightened.

She took a deep breath, and then instead of backing away, she stepped forward, raising her hand to shake one finger at Bill, pitching her voice carefully, choosing her words even more so.

'Now listen, Bill. I don't know what you saw, or thought you saw, and frankly I don't much care,' she said.

She took another step forward, gratified to see him begin to retreat. She had always, as a child, been able to dominate Bill Gunn if she set her mind to it, and now she must be able to. Must!

'Whatever is between Freyn Devereux and me is none of your business, in the first place,' she continued. 'But just for the record I'll tell you that nothing took place last night that I'm the slightest bit ashamed of. Nothing! Do you get that?'

She didn't wait for a reply; she didn't want one.

'Now I'm sorry if you've got the wrong idea, and I'm sorry that you suddenly think so little of me. I would have thought you knew me better than to come here making such foul remarks, but then I thought I knew you better, too. So all I can say now is . . .'

Her voice, now low as she prepared the final

broadside, was interrupted by an equally soft knock at
the door.

'You awake yet, Riley?'

The combatants froze, both looking to the door and
Freyn's second knock. Bill Gunn moved first.

One work-hardened hand caught the front of Riley's
wrapper, then shot forward to fling her backwards
across the bed. Before she could get to her feet, he had
the door open and was leering at the figure who stepped
into the room.

Riley was suddenly all too conscious of Bill's
appearance. His suit looked as if it had been slept in; his
shirt was partly open, the tie knot slipped to gape
widely.

As Freyn entered, eyes registering an appropriate
surprise, Bill stalked confidently out of the room,
fingers raised as he straightened his tie, and marched
away down the corridor.

Freyn said not a single word about the incident, but
that didn't make it better. Riley had seen the shutters
flash across his eyes, seen the ice start to form behind
them.

'I thought you might be game for a swim,' he said.
'But you've obviously already been, so what do you say
to breakfast?'

'I . . . I'll need a minute to change,' she managed to
reply, having to lift each word bodily past the lump in
her throat.

'Fine. How about I meet you in the coffee shop in
fifteen minutes?'

He hardly waited for her nod of acceptance before
turning to stalk out, taking long, angry strides, his back
ramrod-straight, his entire bearing a silent banner of
disapproval.

As the door closed, Riley fought a losing battle
against the tears that flooded her eyes, and the fifteen

minutes stretched to twenty before she had managed, with make-up, to repair the damage.

She entered the coffee shop tentatively, almost afraid to meet Freyn's eyes. What on earth would he be thinking of her now? She wondered. Bad enough after last night, but adding Bill Gunn's personal contribution . . . the only conclusion was total and utter disaster!

Freyn greeted her with a smile. But it was a smile that didn't extend past his gleaming, even teeth. His eyes weren't touched by it at all.

The smile didn't warm up through breakfast, nor did his attitude change throughout the endless day that followed. He was polite, friendly, sometimes even cheerful.

But cold!

And Riley was colder still. Her guilt, however unjustified when looked at from a purely intellectual viewpoint, sat like a lump of ice in her stomach, spreading tendrils of frost throughout her body.

The morning session was too technical for her to have gained much even if she had been interested, which she wasn't. The luncheon froze when it landed on the ice inside her, and the afternoon session of the conference went on and on and on.

'I was going to suggest we try a spot of riding before dinner, but it's too late now,' said Freyn when the final question had been asked and the final speaker droned to a stuttering conclusion.

'It doesn't matter,' Riley replied.

And it didn't. Not when compared to the look in his eyes as he had made the comment. Almost, she thought . . . relief?

'You've held up rather well today,' he said then.

For somebody who spends the early morning in bedroom athletics with a drunk? She didn't say it, but she wanted to. Anger was starting to clear her thinking.

How dared this man patronise her? How dared he so
blatantly put his own interpretation on her actions? He
was no better than Bill Gunn, who would—Riley swore
to herself—pay dearly for what he'd done.

'Last night wasn't an experience I'd care to repeat for
a while,' she said aloud, and then added hurriedly,
'except for the dancing, of course. I really enjoyed that.'

'So did I.'

And what was in that voice now? Regret? Bitterness?
Whatever, it disappeared in his next remark.
'Perhaps we should try the disco tonight, then? Unless
you'd rather have an early night.'

Wishful thinking, Mr Devereux? Riley only just kept
from asking that question aloud. She'd have to watch
herself, she thought.

'An early night seems a bit of a waste,' she said. She
hoped he didn't detect the hopefulness in her voice. 'I
can do that at home.'

'Good thinking. I've booked us into the main
restaurant for dinner in . . . just over an hour,' he said
with a glance at the thin gold watch on his wrist. 'So let's
discuss the alternatives then and see what happens.'

Riley made her own way back to her room, and got a
bleak reception from her bathroom mirror.

A shower, first, she thought. A hot one! Maybe with
any luck she would melt, and resolve at least some of her
problems.

Before she could worry about menu decisions or what
to do with the evening, she had to decide what to wear.
Some choice! It was the evening portion of the ivory
ensemble or . . . Her eyes kept returning to the smoky
blue silk halter-neck.

Did she dare?

'If I don't when will I ever have another chance to
wear it?' she asked the mirror. The mocking, silent
reply was devastating.

'What will he think of me? This dress is indecent.'

'It's beautiful, and you know it. Maybe a little daring, but . . .' replied the devil in her.

'It's practically an invitation to rape!'

'Freyn Devereux wouldn't *have* to rape you.'

'I didn't bring the right eye-shadow. I need a sort of smoky blue colour.'

'Why do you think luxury hotels have shopping facilities?'

'But I . . .'

'Wear it!'

Riley compromised, in the end, by wearing the jacket over the dress, a gesture that gained her exactly nothing.

'You won't need this,' said Freyn after a glance that flashed across her body like a wave of fire.

Strong, lean fingers plucked the jacket from her shoulders and flung it casually over an armchair.

'You're famous for your courage,' he grinned, and when he offered his arm with a nod and a curious raising of one dark eyebrow, Riley gave in. But her courage lasted only to the lobby, where the stares she drew from bystanders made her wish she had listened instead to her common sense.

'I feel as if I'm naked,' she whispered, only to have Freyn laugh without replying. From that instant, things got worse—and better.

The head waiter was experienced enough to cope, but the young man serving their table peered wide-eyed over his order pad and dropped his pencil not once, but twice!

A whispered—too loudly!—remark from a table behind them made Riley want to cringe with embarrassment, and another from two women even further away made her want to stalk over and throw something at them.

But—the gleam of appreciation in Freyn's eyes made

her want to melt.

He devoured her with his eyes throughout the
sumptuous meal, and it was in his gaze that Riley took
shelter from everything else. A dangerous thing to do,
she thought, but the only choice she had. About the only
saving grace was the fact that Bill Gunn wasn't dining
there as well.

'Have some more wine,' Freyn said to her. 'And stop
fretting; you'll give yourself indigestion.'

'After last night, for which I apologise, I'm not sure
more wine is such a good idea.'

'Last night is the past. It's over and done with and
unchangeable. *This* is Piper's Brook wine, which is as
good as anything you'll ever drink in the rest of your
life.'

Over and done with and unchangeable. But not
unforgettable, Riley thought sadly. Like this morning.
She wouldn't forget either of them—one with the
fondest of memories because she had loved the dancing,
and the other—well, just because. If only Freyn could
forget this morning, but he wouldn't.

They spent a long time at dinner, longer than Riley
could ever remember having spent on a single meal. But
it seemed as if Freyn thawed gradually during the meal,
that his eyes lost most of that frosted look, that his
smiles grew warmer, his voice more mellow.

When they finally left, after coffee and liqueurs,
Riley found it easy to walk calmly beside him, ignoring
the jealous glances from other tables, revelling in the
fact that *he* liked her dress, that it obviously gave *him*
pleasure.

She hardly noticed when he turned them not towards
the disco, but into the hotel-casino's gaming rooms.

'You'll have no need to feel self-conscious in here,'
Freyn said with a wry smile. 'Even beauty comes a long
second to the lure of gambling.'

Riley could only smile in return, her eyes already roving the large room. Such excitement, such intensity. But he was right; nobody would notice her dress, or lack of it, here. Everybody was far too intent on the various roulette, blackjack and craps tables.

Freyn excused himself, returning a few minutes later to reach out one hand, fist closed and fingers tucked under. Riley looked at him, then realised she was expected to extend her own hands.

A stream of chips descended into them, along with his comment that, 'This will bring your advance to round figures—easier to remember.'

'You expect me to gamble with this?'

'Why not? You're in hock for so much anyway—what's a few dollars more? Besides, you might just get lucky.'

'Don't hold your breath,' muttered Riley, accepting the chips but wondering if she dared risk even one of them, considering the debts she already had.

And yet . . .

'Why not indeed,' she agreed. And was gladdened by his smile, gratified by his acceptance. If a small flutter was all it took to make him happy, to keep the frost out of his eyes, perhaps erase or fade the memory of this morning's débâcle, why not?

'Good,' he said. 'So what's your pleasure, Miss Jones?'

You! But of course she couldn't say that, shouldn't even dare think it. So she replied, 'Two-up, first, I think. At least I've got some vague idea of what goes on there.'

She left the Two-up school ahead by forty dollars, her eyes bright with excitement and her entire body alive with a feeling of enjoyment.

Roulette, the first time round, cost her dearly, but she regained her losses at the Blackjack table, moved on to

try craps, and almost yelled herself hoarse when it was
her turn to throw the dice. And win. And win again.
And again.

The spinning of the casino-version chocolate wheel
bored her. Keno, she decided, was even worse. So it was
back to the Two-up school, where it seemed for a time
she could do nothing wrong.

She won, won again, and again. Took her turn as the
'spinner' and found she was enjoying the admiring
stares of the male players. And Freyn's glances, which
she noticed even more. Every look was a caress, every
twinkle in those incredible hazel eyes was a
compliment.

Roulette again. Just because she couldn't believe it
was possible never to win at all in the strange game with
its infuriating little bouncing ball.

And she was right. She found a pattern, began to win
again. Her hoard of chips became so big she had to stuff
her evening bag, then had to prevail on Freyn's pockets.

It was like the night before, only without the wine, yet
still she was drunk. Drunk with the excitement, with the
knowledge that somehow this was to be *her* night, her
time to be a winner.

Tomorrow . . . well, she would never, Riley thought,
so much as think of gambling again. This was too heady
an excitement, too risky a pastime. Once was marvellous; twice could too easily be addictive.

In the powder room a few minutes later, she stared
with surprise at the bright-eyed, sparkling creature in
the mirror and then laughed. Delighted. Because that
creature was her, and—more important—was beautiful. And happy.

Still, when Riley returned to the gaming rooms, the
fine edge of the excitement was gone. She determined to
continue until she lost. And at the first loss she would

quit, take her overall winnings, and consider herself lucky indeed.

It took only ten minutes.

She insisted that Freyn allow her to cash in her own chips, and nearly fainted when she reckoned the total.

'I can't believe this,' she said when the wad of bills was folded safely into her evening bag and they'd adjourned to the bar for a much-needed drink.

There was enough money in her handbag to repay Freyn the advance twice over!

'Beginner's luck,' he said with a wide grin. 'Try it again tomorrow, or even in an hour, and you might be surprised.'

'I'd be surprised if I dared *ever* try it again,' Riley replied. 'No way! My frugal ancestors would be horrified.'

'Not to mention your frugal self,' he grinned. 'But just as well; I'd hate to think I was responsible for turning you into a gambling addict.'

'That is one thing you would *never* have to worry about,' she said emphatically. 'And I shall state here and now that if I'd lost the amount you gave me, I should have quit there and then.'

'And I shall state here and now that I believe you. But it was still good fun watching you throwing all your inhibitions away and having such a good time doing it.'

'It was good fun doing that. But now I intend to have even more fun—like repaying the advance you gave me.'

She was already counting out the money when he spoke, and for an instant she didn't catch the seriousness in his voice.

'Already done.'

'But . . . but it can't be. And it won't be, until I give you . . . this.'

'Sorry. Can't take it.'

'But you *have* to take it. Freyn, what are you on about?'

'I won the pittance I advanced you, three times over, by following your lead at the craps table. I've been repaid, so keep your money and enjoy it.'

'But that isn't the same. I can't accept that,' she said, reaching out, the money in her hand.

He refused to take it, and when she tried to stuff it into his pocket, he stopped her with a strength she couldn't match.

'I said that I'm happy to consider my winnings sufficient,' he said.

'Well, that doesn't make me happy,' countered Riley. 'I took your advance, which was bad enough in itself, and I'm going to repay it.'

'Are you always this scrupulous about debts?' he asked, and immediately added, 'No, don't bother to answer because I know you are. But this time, my dear, you must consider yourself defeated. I feel that my winnings are a fair and reasonable repayment, considering that I followed your lead scrupulously, and I will not—*not*—take your money.'

'But ... but can't you see my point at all?' Riley pleaded. 'It ... it just isn't right!'

'Right is right. And if I'm happy, you should be,' Freyn replied with a slow smile. 'Yes, I understand your point; the problem here is that you can't understand mine, because money is far more important to you than it is to me.

'I would have cheerfully bought you those clothes— and especially this dress—because they are so absolutely right for you, and I am more than capable of appreciating beauty for its own sake. But you wouldn't have that, and again I can see your point.

'This way,' he said, with laughter dancing behind his eyes, 'we're both satisfied. Provided of course you'll just ease off a touch on your sense of righteousness.'

'If you'd bought me this dress, I'd feel like a kept woman,' Riley replied. 'It would have taken all the pleasure out of wearing it.'

'Of course. Because you couldn't ever be a kept woman; it isn't your style. But this way, because you were lucky and I rode along on your luck, we're both satisfied. Why not just consider it your lucky dress and be done with it, instead of trying to argue away all the time we should be spending at the disco.'

'I will take the matter under consideration,' she said staunchly. 'And don't think for one minute that this particular discussion is over, because it isn't. I will think about your viewpoint and try to make sense out of it, but if in the end I decide that you'll take the money, you will—if I have to stuff it down your throat.'

'Agreed.' And now his smile was triumphant, if still so warm it threatened to melt her insides. 'Now let's stop bickering over it. We can do that any time; but here and now we should be taking the fullest advantage of what pleasures await.'

He grinned convincingly, and added. 'Which means remembering it's our last night here, and that there's a disco we haven't visited and a show in the cabaret room we haven't seen. Tomorrow morning will be filled with conference wrap-up, so tonight is all there is. Agreed?'

'Agreed,' said Riley, and hoped her eyes didn't reveal the truth of her feelings. If Freyn didn't want to argue over money tonight, she wouldn't argue. If he wanted to go to the disco, or visit the cabaret, or . . . anything, she would go along with him.

Even . . . no, she wouldn't think that far ahead.

The remainder of the evening was a whirlwind of activity. They checked out the cabaret, then went on to the disco. There wasn't a hint of disharmony; not a wrong word between them. Freyn seemed determined

to make their final night in Launceston one to
remember for ever, and he was at his most charming.

For Riley, who started off in a state of mild euphoria
after her casino exploits, the time passed almost as if in
a dream. All thoughts of embarrassment about her
revealing dress were dissipated in the heady acceptance
of Freyn's pleasure in her appearance.

She revelled in his admiring looks—and there were
many. Many from other men in the crowded venues, but
they were irrelevant, merely pale confirmation of the
desire she could see in Freyn's hazel eyes.

When he touched her, regardless of circumstance, her
body sang. She was becoming sensitised to him, attuned
to his moods, his needs, his touch.

When they danced, she couldn't put a foot wrong. If
he reached for her hand, it was already reaching out to
be taken.

The excitement, the crowds, all contributed to their
closeness, and to Riley's pleasure. But really, they were
alone, dancing through a fantasy world of infinite
intimacy, of perfect pleasure.

And when it was time to leave, when Freyn's fingers
touched at her waist and his husky voice whispered that
it was time to go, Riley didn't even think to argue.

They walked down the broad corridor to her room,
hand in hand, their steps co-ordinated, their pace a
curious mixture of haste and leisure. At her room, he
smiled down, took her key, opened the door.

He would come in. She knew he would, and he
obviously knew it too, because no word was spoken,
none was needed. As the door closed, she flowed into his
arms, her lips seeking the touch of his kiss, needing his
kiss.

And she felt a certainty that now all was right, that he
would make love to her as she so desperately wanted
him to, with care and consideration to match the

passion, with a sure and certain knowledge of her needs, even though she herself—in her inexperience—wasn't all that sure of exactly what she needed.

Only of what she wanted!

Her lips parted to receive his kiss, his breath warm and pleasant to taste. Against her body, the strength of him was exciting, arousing. When his lips moved down the long line of her throat, tasting, teasing a trail of desire down to the swell of her breasts, Riley felt a need for more of his kisses, more of his touch.

The thin straps of the halter-neck parted easily beneath his fingers, the dress slipped from her body to flow into a pool of colour at her feet.

She was lifted from the floor, carried over and laid ever so gently on to the bed. She didn't notice if he stepped over the discarded dress, and didn't care. She wrapped her arms around his neck, holding their lips in touch as he discarded his dinner jacket, flinging it behind him to be joined a moment later by his shirt and tie.

Then he was beside her on the bed, his lips joined firmly with her own.

His fingers traced intimate designs along the breadth of her shoulders, down the nubbly track of her spine, into the soft dimpled hollows at its base.

Riley soared as he kissed her again and when his lips moved across her skin, she felt like Icarus nearing the sun. Only her wings didn't melt, she didn't fall; instead she soared higher and higher, her fingers along his neck, down the muscled length of his back.

His lips took her to the sun, but still her melting was controlled, her descent after the explosion slow and delicate, like that of a butterfly.

She felt him vibrate at her touch, not a shivering or shuddering, but the fine pitch of a tuning fork.

His lips moved across her mouth, touched her eyes with gentle persuasion.

'Look at me.'

She met his eyes, her own wide with the delight she saw there, with the empathy, the tenderness and the desire.

His expression was wholly gentle. It was like trying to look through a waterfall, because behind the gentleness was raw, vital, masculine wanting, and her entire being thrilled to it, fought against his verbal restraint.

'Are you sure this is right for you?'

His voice was silk, the words the merest whisper. Lighter even than his touch against her skin.

Riley answered with her lips, but without words. Her mouth lifted to shout her reply, melting to fit the exact contours of his lips.

She felt a mighty gasp rising in his chest, shifted her hand lower to confirm the greatness of his need for her, then let her mind slip all restraint as his fingers plucked desire from her breasts, as his touch moved across her body, readying her, heightening her own need until she thought it could go no higher.

The sunburst of his earlier caresses became as nothing. A mere memory, a tiny part of the universe that now careered into instant detonation at their joining.

Riley's tiny instant of pain was no more than a trigger for the riot of passions that followed as their bodies met and melted and fused.

She was aware of her voice as a soft, soughing wind that occasionally cried out at the peaks of her soaring, plunging journey through ecstasy. She flew to the peaks of fulfilment, plunged away again, returned, crying out her pleasure like the wind from heaven.

She was only dimly aware of him bringing her back from ecstasy, drawing her slowly, gently, caringly back to the reality of his arms, the reality of his lips gentle in aftermath, his touch more so.

'Beautiful.' His voice was feather-soft, repetitive, musical in her ear. 'So beautiful.'

'Beautiful.' Her lips formed round the word, savouring it as her fingers now savoured the touch of his skin, the gradual settling of his breathing against her.

The word became an echo, sliding into sleep with her, drifting through her mind to re-emerge hours later, still coming from the lips that caressed her ear.

'Shall we miss the rest of the conference entirely?' he was saying as she woke the next morning. A long finger reached out to stroke lightly down her cheek, touching briefly at the corner of her mouth. Its path was gentle as a feather, yet to Riley, permanent as a branding iron. She opened her eyes slowly.

'Somebody might notice if we just didn't show up,' she mused, not thinking of anyone in particular.

'Like your little friend Gunn?'

She caught the slight tension in his voice, the shred of ice that accompanied it.

'I wasn't thinking of him.' Truth, because she hadn't, and wouldn't have but for Freyn mentioning it. But now she had, and now she must compound that by remembering the incident only a day before.

Shyness enveloped her, making her feel guilt, and more guilt, shame and more shame.

Without realising it, she was out of the bed, light on her feet as she crossed to the bathroom and locked the door behind her.

The face in the mirror was that of a stranger. Enormous blue-grey eyes stared back at her, eyes no longer innocent but surely not wicked, surely not shamed by memories of such incredible lovemaking?

Her body showed nothing of the night past, no visible

brand to show how Freyn had claimed her so
completely.

'Riley?'

She ignored the light knock at the door, lost in the
mesmerism of trying to outstare her conscience.

'Riley! Are you all right?'

'I'm . . . fine,' she replied, lying now because the eyes
in the mirror had given her the message. Freyn
Devereux had *believed* Bill Gunn's frustrated, bitter
comment! Of course he wouldn't admit it, but that
touch of ice in his voice a minute ago spoke better than
words. He had believed, did believe. This was to be the
end of it, this single night of ecstasy, this one weekend
together.

This naughty weekend, just as he had once promised.

A single tear hovered from a single eyelash, then
splashed down the cheek in the mirror. The face of her
shattered innocence twisted, flowed out of focus as it
was covered by a mist of tears, and Riley turned to stuff
a towel against her teeth, stifling the sound, choking off
the shudders that racked her body.

Only minutes were needed. She fought well and
strongly and managed to stifle the tears before their
tracks were evident on her cheeks. She ran water in the
sink, rinsed her face and eyes quickly, then turned and
grabbed up her wrap from where it hung acros the
shower stall.

'I think I need a swim, a good, long swim,' she said
brightly when she opened the door again and walked
calmly out to meet Freyn.

'You don't think you've had enough exercise? I could
sleep until noon, given the chance.'

His light tone matched her own, but his eyes were
shadowed. Riley shivered inside, but resolved she
couldn't weaken, didn't dare.

'Well, you'll have to do it somewhere else,' she smiled.

'In fact, why don't you? I really would like to . . . to be alone for a bit.'

A clumsy way to say that, perhaps, but Freyn must have heard worse in his time because he didn't argue, didn't make any attempt to draw out her feelings.

It took only a minute after his nodded acceptance and he was at the door, dinner jacket in hand but otherwise fully dressed.

His lips descended to touch lightly at heer own, the kiss devoid of passion now, merely a gesture, she thought.

'I'll see you at breakfast then,' he said. 'In about an hour?'

'About that.' And he was gone.

Riley moved swiftly then. She had to; if she stayed in this room one instant too long she would break down, would give vent to tears that wouldn't stop in an hour, would very likely never stop. And for that she needed the privacy of her own home, of her own surroundings, her own life-style that was so very different from this one.

Into her swim suit, on with the wrapper, grab up the key and she, too, was moving down the morning-quiet corridors of the hotel-casino. This time there was no Bill Gunn to accost her, but the conscience that moved with her shadow was infinitely worse.

CHAPTER EIGHT

MACKIE noticed Riley's subdued mood almost as soon as he got into the logging truck on Monday morning, though to his credit he remained silent about it until they stopped work for lunch.

Even then, he approached the subject with relative caution.

'You seem a bit down,' he said around a mouthful of sandwich. 'Your weekend not go too well?'

Riley took her time before replying, unsure of her ability to find just the right words to ward off further suspicion without blatantly lying in her teeth.

'It was . . . a bit overwhelming, I suppose you'd say,' she finally replied. 'Just so much luxury and excitement . . . and I forgot to tell you—I won heaps and heaps at the casino. Enough to . . . well . . . to pay a few debts, anyway.'

She had almost put her foot in it that time. And she couldn't get involved in explaining about the advance for the clothes, or the shopping trip that followed, or just how influential that trip had been on her weekend.

Nor could she tell him of the horrors of Sunday, only a day behind her and yet seemingly a lifetime away.

Breakfast had been bearable, if a bit strained as both she and Freyn lapsed into studied politeness. Riley knew why she was doing it, but could only presume he was trying to make things easier for her.

The conference sessions, thank heaven, had been interesting and loaded with mind-filling detail. A godsend in helping her to keep her mind off her own inner turmoil.

But the trip home had been a nightmare of inane silences broken by even more inane blurtings of trivia on her part. Freyn at least had the distraction of having to drive, but he, too, seemed thrown off balance by it all.

Was this what love was all about? she wondered.

When they finally arrived back at her cottage, Freyn had been little help at all to her troubled mood. He thanked her for her company, spoke of having enjoyed their time together, offered the information that he would be away most of the week but would try to see her on Friday or Friday night.

She couldn't, in honesty, recall any of his words. Not specifically. Strange, because she could remember the taste of his farewell kiss, remember the gentleness, the warmth of it. But not the words.

They didn't, she had decided later, mean very much anyway except a sort of farewell she could do without.

And as the week passed with no word from Freyn, she became more and more convinced. It was over. It had been nice, perhaps even more than just nice, but it was over.

Her mood deteriorated. She found herself snapping at Mackie for little or no reason, found her judgment going awry. Mackie put up with her until Friday, but that morning phoned with news that she had subconsciously been expecting. At any rate, it didn't surprise her.

'I'm a bit crook,' he said. 'Reckon I've got a touch of the 'flu.' And certainly he sounded it. If Riley hadn't seen his truck at the pub the night before, she would perhaps have been taken in.

'It sounds to me like the kind of 'flu that comes in beercans,' she growled uncharitably. 'I just hope you don't stay exposed to it all weekend, or we'll be in a real fix by Monday.'

His promise to behave sounded hollow, but it wasn't until after she had hung up that Riley began to feel guilty for not allowing him his little pretence.

Generally, he had kept his drinking to a minimum since they had taken on the job at Freyn's, and she had little doubt it was her own bad moods that had forced the little man off the wagon with such a vengeance.

Riley sighed, started to pick up the telephone to call and apologise, then shrugged off the impulse. It wouldn't accomplish anything in the long run, she thought.

Besides, the day could be put to good use without going to the bush. She ate her breakfast, idly planning how she would spend the morning servicing the log truck, then go to the city in the afternoon to get some parts she had ordered for the bulldozer.

She might even, Riley considered, stay over for tea and maybe a film. Anything to avoid the remote possibility of having to face Freyn Devereux, although she realised logically that such an attitude was stupidity itself. She would have to meet him sooner or later, and the fact that she didn't really expect him to arrive today as he'd said meant little in the long term.

And what difference could it make if he was there in person or not? He'd already taken up permanent residence in her mind. And her heart.

Which, she thought later that day, was at least some sort of excuse for her driving through the historic subdivision of Battery Point, her eyes scanning the street numbers to find the block of flats where he lived.

It didn't take long to find the place, nor was she surprised by the waterfront location, with its exceptional views of the Derwent estuary and the Tasman Bridge.

And having found it—now what? Riley circled the block, then parked several buildings away and just sat there, staring absently.

'I must be mad,' she muttered to herself. 'This is accomplishing absolutely nothing. I'm just torturing myself, that's all.'

She reached out to the ignition key, then found herself frozen in that position as her eyes focused on the blonde-haired figure emerging from the building.

Clarice Downs! No doubt about it, no possible question. Riley watched as the blonde, immaculate as usual, strode up to an expensive sports sedan, her arms filled with what appeared to be clothing.

It *was* clothing. More significant, it was clearly some man's clothing. Freyn's?

Riley averted her head as Clarice returned to the flats for another load. Her heart was thundering, her eyes locked to the doorway until the blonde emerged once more.

Clarice Downs doing Freyn's laundry? More likely his dry-cleaning, she thought, from the look of the garments. Not that it mattered; what *did* matter was that the blonde was clearly ensconced in Freyn's life.

While she, Riley thought bitterly, was nothing more than a casual plaything, a project he had evolved into its ultimate sexual conclusion.

She watched as Clarice drove away, then sat staring at the vacant parking space, her throat working to hold down the feeling of sickness.

What a fool! What an utter, complete, stupid fool she had been. She had walked into the situation with her eyes wide open, ignoring Mackie's spoken words and Julius Gunn's unspoken but equally obvious advice. No wonder Bill had been so angry; her stupidity must have been blatantly obvious.

But how was she to know? She had never been here to this flat, never so much as telephoned.

Nor, she suddenly realised, had she ever been invited. Not that it was difficult to realise why. She found herself then wondering what kind of woman Clarice Downs must be, for surely the blonde must have anticipated what could happen when Riley and Freyn went off to the conference?

On the other hand, what had Clarice been up to while they were gone? Very likely, Riley thought, the blonde and Freyn had one of those thoroughly modern 'arrangements' that allowed for such things.

And she felt even sicker.

How, she wondered, could people live like that? Riley didn't consider herself a prude, despite being slightly naïve, but she could not conceive of herself being involved in such a relationship.

Especially, she decided with sudden vengeance, as a third party!

She turned on the ignition, drove away from Battery Point as quickly as the narrow, usually charming, streets would allow, and back into the crowded streets of the city itself. She daren't go home now, just on the vague possibility that Freyn might actually come seeking her. She couldn't face him. Not now. She wasn't even sure she could face herself. How could she have so naïvely let herself be lured into that weekend of temptation?

'Because I wanted to,' she said aloud. 'I wanted to, and I knew he did too. But what a stupid, wilful thing to do!'

Especially, she thought, considering that she was forced by necessity to maintain a working relationship with Freyn, and would be forced to maintain it for quite some time to come.

'Which means I'd better get my act together, and damned soon, too,' she told herself. 'After all, it's not the end of the world. I certainly can't be the first girl ever to make a fool of herself over a man.'

That decison made, she drove out to Moonah for a lonely but somehow quite satisfying Chinese feast at the Hong Kong, opted to forget about the movie, and instead spent the evening window-shopping. She was home by ten and in bed asleep less than an hour later, to her relief without any sign of Freyn Devereux. On Saturday, Riley was up with the dawn and busy honing her axe on a hand-driven whetstone when he arrived.

'You look industrious. Don't you ever take a day off?' he said, alighting from his car with a broad smile.

'I'm a working girl; I don't have time for days off,' Riley replied, not quite meeting his look. She was calm, determined to keep herself aloof but polite.

'I suppose that means I'd be wasting my time inviting you for a drive in the country then? I rather fancied a day playing tourist.'

Temptation reared like a swaying cobra, but Riley forced herself to a gentle but firm reply. She must not succumb!

'If I didn't have this axe to finish, and then two chainsaws to pull apart and service, and my laundry to do, and the house to clean, and . . .'

'I got the message,' he interjected. The cloud across his eyes matched the coldness of his voice. Riley hated herself, momentarily, but quickly shrugged off the feeling. It was a luxury she daren't afford herself; she was vulnerable enough as it was.

'This is all relative to last weekend, isn't it?' he asked then. 'Which is understandable, I suppose, except that I can't understand why we can't talk about it.'

'There isn't anything to talk about,' she replied with as much coolness as she could manage. 'It happened and that's all there is to it. I'm not blaming you, if that's what worries you.'

'What worries me has nothing to do with blame,' Freyn replied. 'I think I'd rather have you blaming me than shrugging the whole thing off so casually.'

'Well, what would you have me do . . . weep and wail and tear my hair? What's done is done, and I have no intention whatsoever of wallowing in it, if you don't mind.'

Riley turned her attention back to her gleaming axe blade at that point. Such brave words, considering that wallowing in it was exactly what she had been doing for the last week.

She concentrated on turning the grindstone, watching the shining steel as she prepared the razor-edge she wanted on the axe. But Freyn didn't speak, and eventually his silence forced her to pause, to look up at him.

She met eyes grim as death. Cold eyes, diamond-hard in their bitter stare. She wavered, inwardly, before their assessment. Outwardly, she stayed cool.

'Was there something else?'

'You might tell me why you've decided to become so ... so distant. But I suppose you won't.'

No, she thought, I won't. Because that would mean revealing how I feel, because I'd have to mention Clarice Downs, which would mean admitting that I ...

'I think you're making altogether too much of the whole thing,' she replied coolly. 'It was a wonderful weekend; we both had a good time, and no, I'm not interested in a repeat performance, thank you.'

Liar! She'd repeat the performance at a moment's notice, given just the slightest indication that it mattered to him, that there was some element of love involved.

Because that was the one thing missing. Freyn, even at the height of passion, had never, ever, spoken of love. And Riley now realised that for her part, love was the foundation stone of everything between she and Freyn. But it couldn't be unrequited love—she couldn't live with that.

There was nothing to be gained by dissecting the memories of that weekend one by one, most especially

not with Freyn Devereux in charge of the dissection. He
was much too astute; he would see through her in a
minute.

'Well, I guess that's that, then,' he was saying, and his
voice was as cold as death, as cold as his eyes. 'I'm
pleased you had a good time.'

He turned away, striding back to his car in long,
angry strides. Riley could have wept, but for her own
protection she pretended not even to notice when he
drove off, and didn't so much as look up.

Which made it difficult, because it meant that she
didn't know if he had even bothered to look back. And
she wanted to know, very much so. Now that he was
gone, she could admit that to herself, she supposed.

Doing so did little to improve her temperament, and
Mackie's continuing 'illness', which prevented him
from turning up for work on Monday, meant she did
even less.

She wouldn't, of course, attempt any tree felling. Not
on her own. But she could get a load of logs.

Riley had often said that machinery was invented to
make work easier. Today wouldn't be the first time she
had put the thought into practice. She had often loaded
the truck entirely by herself, and had no qualms about
doing so again. The fact that on previous occasions her
off-sider had at least been within shouting distance . . .
well . . . she could ignore that.

And did!

Loading was, in fact, remarkably easy. They had a
good stockpile of logs, the skidder made the job
relatively simple, and her own bad temper overcame
any qualms she might have had concerning safety or the
lack of it.

The problem was that it took her only two hours to get
a load on the jinker, get the binding chains in place, and
cinch them down with a series of load-binders. Having

done all that, she was ready to leave for the mill whenever she wanted, and there was most of the day yet ahead of her.

She spent until noon measuring the logs that remained, using a simple formula involving length and mid-point girth to tell her the cubic metre content of each log. Then she had lunch, and rested in the warm sunshine.

She pondered the risk of getting in some more logs, then discarded the idea as downright stupid. The trees she had in mind were safe enough to work with, but she couldn't force herself to reject the first rule ever laid down for her by her late father.

'You do not and will not ever go felling timber alone,' he had said.

If she had been working for one of the big companies, she knew, just the situation of having loaded the truck by herself would be grounds for instant sacking; to go off cutting trees by herself would be considered insanity.

Of course she could bring it off—but if something went wrong . . . It didn't take much of a mistake to have death as the penalty.

Every independent contractor did it at some time, of course, she told herself. Then, wisely, she thought of the ones who had put themselves into graves or wheelchairs for their folly.

No, best to take the sensible path. She would continue her exploration of Freyn's timber tract. That was safe.

Two hours later she wasn't so sure. She had lost her footing while working down into a gully where there looked to be an excellent stand of big stringy-barks, and the resulting descent—razor-sharp axe in hand—had left Riley somewhat shaken.

She'd lost the skin off one palm, ripped half the

bottom out of her jeans, twisted one ankle and muddied
and ripped her shirt.

Not to mention scaring herself quite thoroughly into
the bargain. Still, she thought once the trembling was
under control, the trees would make excellent logs if she
could find a route to get her machinery in to them.

Then she tried to walk, and immediately realised that
finding a route to get herself *out* had become an issue of
far greater significance. While she had been lying back
admiring the timber, her ankle had begun to swell
inside her boot, a certain indication that her ankle
might be more than just twisted.

She glared at the offending foot, cursed, then sank
back in agony after yet another attempt to put her full
weight on it. Riley began to worry in earnest now. This
was serious.

She rested a few minutes, then used the axe as a prop
to get her upright. The first few hobbling steps threw
piercing pains through her ankle; it was as if the joint
was filled with broken glass.

But gradually the pain eased, and although she
couldn't let the ankle take her full weight, she could
hobble along by using the axe as a walking stick.

'And if I fall, it had better be well away from the axe,
or I'll slice my leg off and finish things off well and
truly,' she told herself sternly.

The journey back to the log landing was a nightmare.
She was unable to climb back out of the gully to where
there was a navigable trail, but had to constantly work
her way across the slope, angling down the gully and
taking frequent rests as she travelled.

Riley cursed as she went along. She cursed herself for
being so clumsy. Bill Gunn for his interference, for the
way he had poisoned her weekend, and she cursed
Freyn Devereux for everything.

Only Mackie, whose wizened, grizzled face she would

give anything to see right now, escaped her wrath. And that despite Mackie's absence having led to this predicament.

Her ankle had swollen to fill the boot, which if nothing else helped give her more stability, allowed her to move with slightly less pain. But still her travel was excruciatingly slow; she would be lucky to make the truck before dark, Riley thought.

Her circuitous route was adding to the delay, but she was too far along it now to even contemplate trying to climb up to the ridge, because that trail—if her memory of the map was correct—had already veered far off to her left. She would have to negotiate through bush as untravelled as where she was, with less certainty of finding her way.

She used her next rest break to sprawl flat on her back, mind trying to conjure up a true picture of the aerial photograph she had thought she'd memorised. This gully, if memory served, would begin to flatten out soon. Or did it? Maybe she was in the *next* gully, which wouldn't begin to level out until she was far past the landing.

Worse, her exhaustion was beginning to make thinking difficult. She could get the picture in her mind, but it then began to flicker, contour lines merging into a muddle of confusion.

Off to her right, a kookaburra screamed, and the maniacal laughter seemed to be a personal insult to her own stupidity.

In the other direction, a mob of currawongs began their uncanny, mechanical conversation as they swirled through the forest.

'Clink clink. Clink clink. Clink clink.' It was a sound so artificial, so utterly unbirdlike. And now, so menacing, as the echoes emphasised how alone she was.

And further in the distance, a raven sounded his sad,

wavering call, the drawn-out 'waaauuugh' not at all conducive to peace of mind.

Riley thought of getting up, then closed her eyes and voted for a few minutes more rest. There was still time to get out before dark, provided she didn't do something totally stupid, like getting properly lost.

She remembered her father recounting a similar adventure of his own, years before, and the comment that he never got lost. 'I always knew where I was; it was the truck that was lost,' he'd said. And he had laughed, because such an adventure—once safely done—was a legitimate source of bush humour.

She rested, moved on, rested again. The effort was costing her; she didn't think she was tracking properly, but had no choice but to keep going at least until closer to full dark.

If she didn't make it out—well, too bad. She had an axe, matches, and a night without food wouldn't kill her, she thought.

'Good for keeping the old figure nice and slim. Men like girls to be slim.' She found herself repeating the second sentence over and over as she hobbled along, and vowed to stop, though she didn't.

The wailing raven had circled closer, now, and the clinking currawongs had taken his place in the distance, their noise startling, like somebody beating on a steel drum, or bashing on the side of a truck.

Then another noise began to intrude, and it was so like the raven's wail in her mind that she didn't pick it up, at first. When she did, Riley stopped dead, ears pricked to the direction from which the sound came.

Again. And again, so that she was certain. Somebody was sounding the horn of the logging truck, and from the direction she could orientate herself easily.

She had got into the second gully. And the landing was off to her left. If she kept going, she would

eventually come out in the far corner of the paddocks
that surrounded Freyn's aunt's cottage, but it was the
long way round and no question.

'Damn,' she muttered, and looked to her left for some
easy way of negotiating the slope that would carry her
over the ridge and on to the track she'd made during the
previous week.

Guided by the steady sounding of the horn, she tried
to speed up her pace. Then, having fallen twice and
nearly cut her fingers off with the axe, she slowed it
again and gradually found her way up to the ridge and
the heaven-blessed track.

From that point, it was all downhill, but manoeuvring
in the rough bulldozer tracks proved almost as difficult
as making her way through the bush, where at least she
had been able to grab at trees and bushes for support.

She was still drawn by the horn, sounding in steady
one-two-three blasts, followed by a short pause. It would
be Mackie, she thought, although for the life of her she
couldn't imagine why he should be there.

Only, when she lurched round the final bend, when
she could see the loaded jinker and the figure that stood
half in and half out of the cab, punching angrily at the
horn button while scanning the surrounding bush, it
wasn't Mackie at all.

It was Freyn Devereux, for once totally out of context
in his city business suit and for once looking as if he
wasn't totally in control of the situation.

Freyn! Riley took in his frazzled appearance as he
dropped down from the truck at his first sight of her, as
he plunged through the litter and mud of the landing
with no apparent thought for his quite unsuitable shoes
and clothing.

Unconsciously, her back straightened, her tiredness
was swept away by the need for control, the need to
reduce the stupidity of this afternoon into something

she could manage, could defend.

'My God,' he cried as he reached her. 'What have you been doing to yourself, woman?'

'Oh, don't go on,' she replied. 'I had a bit of a spill, that's all.'

'A bit of a spill? You look like something the cat dragged in at midnight.'

'Well, thank you very much. You, of course, are the image of sartorial splendour,' she retorted peevishly.

'What are you on about?' he shouted. 'And more to the point, what in heaven's name are you doing wandering around out here alone. Where's your helper, what's-his-name?'

'Sick,' she replied, honestly enough. 'He's sick. Got a bug or something.'

'Well then, who loaded this truck?'

'I did, of course. What do you think I am ... helpless?'

She got that line out beautifully, then blew the whole thing by trying to take one simple step forward, revealing her limp and almost falling flat on her face.

Freyn reached out to grab for her, nearly losing a finger as she jabbed with the axe handle to catch her balance.

'Damn it!' he cried, reaching out to pluck the axe from her fingers and fling it aside as he caught her in his arms, lifting her like a child.

'Put me down, Freyn!' Riley began immediately to kick and wriggle against his grasp, anger dominating her weariness.

'Be quiet,' he replied, turning to pick his way carefully across the bark-strewn landing. He used sheer strength to nullify her wriggling objections, and finally reached a bare, relatively clean section of log beside the truck.

Easing Riley into a sitting position, he maintained his

grip until sure she could keep her balance, then stepped back to glare angrily at her.

'You're a stupid, stupid woman!' he charged. 'And I suppose having a totally unnecessary sprained ankle won't make you admit it.'

'It isn't sprained. If it was sprained I wouldn't have been able to walk at all,' she replied defensively. 'I've twisted it; that's all.'

'And of course you wouldn't have any elastic bandage or anything approaching a first-aid kit in the truck?'

'In the glove box,' she muttered, knowing he would find it soon enough by himself anyway, or else improvise.

'Marvellous.' But his voice was still caustic.

His fingers, however, were strangely gentle as he worked her boot off and, after a cursory inspection of her ankle, he began to wrap it in elastic bandage. He undertook the task with the confidence of someone who'd done such things before.

Riley wasn't impressed, or if she was, had no intention of admitting it.

'You shouldn't have taken my boot off,' she snarled. 'I'm going to have the devil's own time getting it back on, now.'

'Good. It'll save you trying to do anything else stupid,' he replied without a hint of humour.

'You expect me to drive this truck with one foot bare?'

'I don't expect you to drive it at all,' he replied, and without warning, reached out to capture her good leg and remove the boot from that foot, as well.

Even as Riley squeaked with surprise, he flung both boots up into the yawning cab of the truck, then rose to stand looming over her like some avenging angel. One hand flickered inside his coat to emerge in a tinkle of keys—her keys, she realised, from the truck—which he waved at her just out of reach.

'So you don't waste your energy trying to climb up there,' he said. 'I'll have to walk down and get the car; it'll be a sight easier than carrying you all the way back to the house.'

'I should hope so! But you don't have to carry me anywhere,' she retorted, her face flushed with anger. How dared he take over her life yet again? Did he think she was totally helpless, absolutely inadequate?

'Of course I don't. I could just leave you here,' he replied. 'Speaking of which . . .' He clambered up into the truck again to emerge shaking her vacuum flask, which from the sound still held some of her lunch-time tea.

'Just the thing,' he grunted as he descended once more with the flask in one hand and Riley's jacket in the other. He wrapped the jacket round her shoulders, then poured her a cup of tea and smiled to see that it was still hot enough to steam in the cooling evening air.

'Get that into you; it might soothe your temper a bit,' said Freyn. 'I won't be any longer than I have to be.'

'Wait. Wait, Freyn.'

He paused, already turned away to leave.

'Will you please go and get me my axe, while it's still light enough to find it?' Riley tried to keep the request polite, forced herself to throttle the growing anger at Freyn's high-handed takeover.

'Your axe? What are you going to do with that?' he replied.

'Oh, cut down a tree or two while you're gone; what do you think?' she snapped peevishly. 'I'm going to put it away, of course. I can't leave it lying there, can I?'

'I cannot imagine why not,' he replied, but altered his departure path and returned a moment later with the axe carried lightly in one strong hand. He carefully laid it across the truck seat, then turned and bowed.

'Now, is there anything else Madam would like before I depart on my mission of mercy?'

'You could try just giving me back my truck keys,' Riley retorted. 'I'm perfectly capable of driving home on my own, whether you think so or not. And besides, I've got a load of logs to deliver, in case you hadn't noticed.'

'In the dark? Because in case *you* hadn't noticed, my dear Miss Jones, it's going to be dark very soon.'

Riley shook her head in dismissal. Was there never any sense in arguing with this man? Of course there was no great panic in getting the truck back; the mill would be closed down already for the day, much less by the time she could get there.

Freyn smiled at her acquiescence, but it was a cold, hard smile. There was no friendliness in it.

'Don't go away,' he ordered, and walked off towards the track to the cabin. Infuriating as his departing comment had been, Riley was even more indignant at the fact that he walked off whistling—and didn't even bother to look back.

She finished off the tea while she waited, scheming in frustration because much as she would have liked to climb into the truck and hot-wire the ignition, thus allowing her to totally disobey Freyn, there wouldn't be time and she didn't—not really—believe she could drive effectively with one foot wrapped in an elastic bandage.

Nor was there time. He returned so quickly that she thought he must have trotted all the way to the cabin, and it was no consolation when he emerged from the car carrying a blanket in which to wrap her.

CHAPTER NINE

'DON'T you think you're carrying this just a bit far? There's nothing wrong with me but a twisted ankle. I'm not an invalid!'

Writhing in Freyn's arms for the third time in less than an hour, Riley might as well have talked to the rising moon for all the good her arguments did her.

She endured his silence for perhaps three seconds, then began another impassioned plea. 'And I don't want to be here; why can't you just drive me home if you insist on being such a do-gooder?'

'I can listen to your whingeing just as well here,' he replied, voice muffled by the blanket which had now twisted round to cover her entirely.

'And can you explain what's going on to whoever comes looking for me? Because they will, you know?'

'Oh, I don't think so.'

He was pushing open the door to his aunt's cabin now, using one knee and precariously balanced due to Riley's continuing struggles.

'Stop that wriggling, will you? You're worse than carrying a bagful of puppies.'

Riley didn't stop, didn't dare. She could *not* let this happen. She didn't want to be alone with him in the bush, much less in his car, and most certainly not here! 'Julius was expecting those logs today,' she lied. 'When I don't show up, he'll reckon something's wrong and send somebody out looking for me.'

'Uh-huh.' He didn't sound at all convinced.

'Well, he will! And when he does, I'm half inclined to scream abduction, or . . . or . . . rape!'

'Lots of luck.' And he dropped her into one of the huge armchairs near the blessed warmth of the fire he had obviously started when he returned for his car.

The slight jar sent stabbing pains up her ankle, but Riley fought back a cry. She would not admit to this beastly, overbearing man how much it hurt her.

'If I'd known you were going to be such a fool, I'd have brought along more food,' he said then, turning away to glare into the emptiness of the refrigerator, which wasn't even turned on.

'But I didn't, so it'll have to be steak, medium-rare, and spuds, baked. No veggies, no salad, but there's some wine, which should compensate.'

Riley was genuinely startled. What on earth was Freyn doing driving all this way with such foodstuffs in his car? Then she thought again. Either he had brought the food for himself, or had merely stopped on his way home, where the missing aspects of the meal would of course be supplied.

By Clarice Downs, no doubt.

'I don't want to deprive you of your dinner,' she replied, hoping the first possibility was the right one.

'You won't. I had a big lunch in the city, so I won't need much.'

He was already unpacking the cooler—when had he brought that in?—and in the soft light from the fire she fancied his anger was softening, even if hers wasn't.

'I would rather just go home,' she said in one final attempt to make Freyn change his mind.

'And I'd rather you didn't,' he replied calmly. 'Now why don't you just settle down and enjoy the fire? As soon as I've got this organised I'll have a decent look at your ankle and wrap it up properly.'

'My ankle is just fine,' she replied, fighting to keep her own voice as calm as his. 'It's just that I . . . I don't want to be found here, like this, when they come looking for me.'

He hadn't really answered her earlier accusations in that regard, nor did he this time.

'I wouldn't worry about it,' he said.

'You don't have to worry; it isn't your reputation,' she argued.

Freyn, by this time, had turned away and was standing by the sink with a potato in one hand and the peeler in the other.

'We could have them fried, if you'd rather,' he said. 'Or boiled, but only if you insist.'

'Freyn—that isn't an answer,' Riley cried.

'Neither is that. Come on—baked, boiled or fried?'

Her reply was uncomplimentary to both potato and chef.

Freyn put everything down, wiped his hands carefully, then stalked over to stand above her, eyes glaring down with menace.

'You didn't talk like that during our weekend away together,' he said in a voice so soft she could barely make out the words. 'Not once! What is it with you— the clothes or something? You put on a pair of jeans and a flannel shirt and you're a different person!'

For once, she had no reply. Not that he seemed to care; without waiting for an answer, he turned and walked back to the sink, where he resumed scrubbing the potatoes without so much as looking at her.

Riley, stunned by the vehemence of his accusation, huddled in the chair and watched. It was a low blow, she thought, or would have been if it hadn't been so true.

'I don't do it with anybody else.'

She gasped with the realisation of having spoken aloud, but he gave no sign of having heard her.

It was true, though, she told herself. Nobody else possessed the ability to provoke her beyond all control, beyond all the bounds of logic and manners and common sense. Only Freyn Devereux.

Because it was only Freyn Devereux that she loved. Any other man—all other men—had no ability to touch her at all. Even in her justifiable anger at Bill Gunn, she hadn't lost control, hadn't even come close.

But Freyn, with far less provocation, could make her lose her temper in an instant with no more than a touch, a look, a word.

His preparations over, he shifted the meat and potatoes away from the sink and ran it full of hot, soapy water. Then he returned to gaze down at Riley, who was too shamed to meet his eyes.

'You'll want to clean up before dinner, I reckon,' he said, leaning down to take her hand. 'And since you insist you can walk, you might as well give it a try.'

He helped her to limp over to the sink, brought her a fresh towel and a chair to lean on. Lifted the blanket from around her shoulders.

'I'll be outside,' he said. 'Call if you need me, or when you're done, and I'll give your ankle another wrap-up and then get started on tea.'

Obviously not needing a reply, he left without meeting Riley's eyes, without even looking at her.

Alone, she stared into the mirror above the sink and recoiled with disgust. No wonder he didn't want to look at her! Her face was grimy with dust and scratches, her hands far more so. She looked like some kind of tramp, the kind who hadn't washed since last spring.

'Yuk! I'll need more than just a wash to get rid of this,' she said half-aloud. 'I need a bath, maybe two baths.'

And found herself thinking irreverently of being stretched out in a huge marble bath-tub, with scented, bubbly water and Freyn Devereux to scrub her back.

Riley shook her head, dispersing the vision. Then she

set to and began repairing the damage as best she could.
It took her the best part of half an hour, and three fresh
sinks full.

Stripping off her torn shirt, she was able to give
herself a reasonable sponge bath from the waist up, but
to get her jeans off required a bit of contortionism that
proved almost beyond her. She finally managed it,
though, and it was worth the effort to be able to feel
thoroughly clean. Now if she only had some clean
clothes to put on, too, instead of replacing the filthy
work gear . . .

'Aren't you finished yet? It's getting cold out here!'
Freyn's voice thundered through the door, startling
Riley so badly she almost fell.

'I'm just getting dressed again. I won't be a minute,'
she called back, then grabbed for the blanket in panic as
the door was flung open.

'You're not putting that dirty stuff back on. Hang on
a minute and I'll get you something that's at least clean,
even if it might not fit too well.'

'But . . . but I'm . . .' Naked, because the blanket was
just out of reach and it was too late anyway, he was
already inside.

'I know, but if you close your eyes I won't be
embarrassed,' he said in a voice thick with suppressed
laughter. Which she actually did, until the ridiculous-
ness of the suggestion got through to her weary,
exhausted brain. Then she turned around with the soap
in her upraised hand, only to find he was too close to
throw it at.

'You . . .'

'You didn't do your hair. Do you want a hand with
it?' he said, eyes steadfastly fixed above her forehead.

His outstretched hands held a shirt of soft, quality
flannel, obviously his own and so big it would fit Riley
like a tent. Held as he did, however, it effectively

concealed her from his gaze, which now met her eyes in
a curious mixture of seriousness and laughter.

She couldn't endure it, and instead turned around so
as to slip her arms into the upheld shirt. As she had
suspected, it covered her from neck to knees, which was
a blessing in the circumstances.

'I can't imagine you in the hairdressing business,' she
said softly, still not turning to face him. 'And it isn't that
bad, really.'

'It's filthy and you know it,' he growled, taking her
shoulders and turning her, but gently, giving her plenty
of opportunity to adjust her balance. 'Now stop being so
hard to get along with. I'll do your hair and then fix up
your ankle again—I see you managed to wash it all
right—and then we'll see about getting around some
dinner, because I've discovered I'm famished after all.'

He waited until she was steadied over the sink, hair
awash with suds as his fingers scrubbed through it,
before explaining his unexpected hunger.

'I reckon it was all this business of carrying you
around that's raised my appetite,' he said. 'You're a lot
heavier than you look, even with your boots off.'

Riley, eyes squinched shut to avoid the suds that
seemed to have engulfed her head, could say nothing,
which was obviously what he had intended.

'I really ought to fire you, you know! Or should have,
right on the spot. Of all the damned fool things to do,
wandering around by yourself with nobody knowing
where to even start looking.

'If you hadn't already done yourself such an injury,
my girl, I can tell you now that you wouldn't be sitting
down for dinner tonight; you'd be standing up for a
week.'

Riley gasped, then began to splutter at the taste of
soapy water she had inhaled in the process. Freyn's
laughter seemed to come from a distance, although she

could still feel his fingers gently massaging her scalp.

'That'll teach you', he chuckled.

She tried to kick him in response, but just in time realised she was balanced on her good leg and would pay a dear price if she kicked him with her already injured ankle.

He continued lathering her hair for a moment longer, chuckling as he did so. It was infuriating, especially as she couldn't see him because she didn't dare open her eyes. He was using soap on her hair, having explained that the place didn't usually run to shampoo.

'Okay, get yourself well braced now, because I'm about to give you the first rinse,' he said after another long period of silence.

Riley did do, still balancing on one foot but carefully so, with both hands firmly on the edge of the sink and her head dipped low so as to keep the shirt dry.

What followed was agony! Freyn Devereux, the pig, dumped half a bucket of absolutely ice-cold water over her head, and stood there laughing as she gasped in shock.

'More?' he asked as she half turned, killing him with her eyes, the freezing water streaming down her face.

Riley said nothing, snatched at the towel and began to scrub at her hair. It was so short that the single rinse was enough three times over, and well he knew it, she thought. But if he thought he would have the satisfaction of hearing her complain, much less curse him as he deserved, well ... he had another think coming.

'Thank you very much,' she said once she had managed to still the shivering. 'That was very stimulating; just what I needed. Now if you'd remembered to bring in my handbag from the truck ...' And she stopped, because there it was, sitting right on the drainboard in front of her.

She stifled the words, fumbled inside for her brush and comb, and turned away from Freyn to face herself in the mirror, to try and straighten up the mess she must look.

It should have worked, but it didn't. She found his glance, one eyebrow mocking raised, only served to make it more difficult for her. She brushed at her hair, trying to obliterate his reflection with careful movements of her elbow, but it didn't really work.

In the mirror, his eyes glowed. His personality seemed to take command despite being only a reflection, he showed that astonishing ability to see right through her, to virtually read her mind.

Even as she watched, for some reason unable to move, his fingers reached out to touch at the damp mop of hair that sat at her nape. They squeezed out the dampness, then moved that fraction lower to begin massaging the warm skin at the top of her spine.

Riley stared into the mirror, her eyes begging him to stop, her mouth poised in a slightly breathless pause that exposed just the tips of her teeth.

In the mirror, their eyes locked, and her plea for him to stop softened, flickered, spun in confusion before submitting to her inner desire for him never to stop, for him to keep his fingers on her for ever and for ever.

Whereupon he did stop, and she saw the glimmer of satisfaction in his eyes as he did so. He knew! He knew full well the effect he had been having on her!

'I think we'd better think about some food pretty soon,' he said, 'but first I'd better look at getting that ankle bound up again.'

'I can do it myself,' she snapped. Peevish, now. Angry at him for using his charms so blatantly, so deliberately. So—callously.

'You'll do as you're told.' Something in his voice cautioned her against objection. She allowed him to help her back to the armchair, sat there quietly while he prepared two buckets—one filled with hot water, the other with cold.

'Each as long as you can possibly stand it, while I get the potatoes going,' he said. 'And no cheating, because I'll be watching.'

'I don't cheat!'

A stupid reply, one she needn't have bothered with. It gained her only a sardonic look in which one raised eyebrow said everything without words.

He moved away, and Riley found herself gritting her teeth in agony as she poised her foot over the first bucket and then plunged it in. Agony? It was that and worse. The water seemed to grind the glass within her ankle; she watched her skin turn pink, then lobster-red.

And when she switched from hot to cold, it was worse, at least at first. She had to bite back a cry, keep her teeth clenched against the moans that birthed deep in her chest and fought their way up through a shuddering passage to lodge against her teeth.

The second time was easier. The third, bearable. Now her problem was the smell of the potatoes gently sizzling in the large cast-iron frying pan.

She closed her eyes, let the warmth of the fire flow into her body, and tried to forget about her foot and which bucket it might now be in.

'Here. This'll make it easier.'

She opened her eyes, took the glass of white wine with fingers that trembled slightly. And noticed that he noticed, that he was aware of how much she was suffering.

One long-fingered hand dipped into the hot bucket, withdrew after a gasp she would have turned to a scream.

'Are you mad, woman? Why didn't you tell me it was so hot?'

'I thought you'd tested it.' And she had, though that was no excuse.

'I did,' he admitted, and had the grace to look slightly sheepish. 'But obviously not well enough. You'll have blisters as well as a sprained ankle.'

'It's all right now.' she assured him. 'And it isn't sprained, it's just a bit twisted, that's all. It would be fine by tomorrow without all . . . this.'

'Maybe,' he replied, gently drying off her foot with fingers that seemed like moth's wings against the tender skin. Then he was wrapping on the elastic bandage again, a clean, new one, this time.

'Where did that come from?' The words emerged even as she thought.

'Santa Claus.'

Riley almost giggled. She took another gulp of the wine, noticed the glass was now empty, and blinked at the tiny explosion it all made inside her.

'You're not much of a barmaid,' she said, laughing at the thought of Freyn Devereux in apron and mini-skirt, dispensing drinks behind the bar of some country pub.

He finished the bandaging, rose to take the glass with a grin. 'One more, and that's all you get before we eat,' he replied. 'Besides, I wouldn't mind having some left for me. I've done all the work, after all.'

His smile was a breath of warm, fresh air.

Riley sat and stared into the fire, only occasionally turning her head to look at where Freyn loomed over the old woodstove, his face sheathed in shadow as he watched the steaks cooking.

Under the window, the table was already set with the mis-matched china and cutlery his aunt had bequeathed him, and instead of expensive wine there was only a cardboard cask of Moselle, but to Riley's eyes it was perfection in itself. She had discarded the blanket, and sat now covered only by Freyn's soft flannel shirt; she was too warm even in that, because he had heaped the fireplace high.

As he dished the meal on to two old china plates and beckoned to her, she rose and hobbled to the table, her ankle, surprisingly, much better for his harsh ministrations.

He refilled her glass, then his own, and the two of them began eating immediately and in silence. Freyn must have lied about the size of lunch he had had, Riley decided, judging by the way he devoured the enormous steak. For her own part, she needed no excuse, and matched him bite for bite.

It was ambrosia, truly a meal from heaven.

'I reckon there's not much sense taking you off to fancy casinos for a weekend,' he said after the initial appetite had been vanquished. 'You look like you're enjoying that better than anything you ate in Launceston.'

'Maybe it's more my style,' she replied cautiously, not willing to admit that fact directly.

'Meaning you didn't enjoy the weekend?'

'Meaning I didn't enjoy the food as much as this. But then I wasn't as hungry as this, either.'

'That's not what I meant.'

'I know what you meant.'

He looked at her, eyes blazing with . . . what was it? Then he spoke, and his voice was strangely soft, yet seemed to ring in her ears.

'Okay.' And he raised his glass. 'To us!'

Riley froze. Pondered. Tried to read his eyes, but couldn't.

How could he expect her to drink to *them*? Surely he must know her well enough to know she couldn't, wouldn't be content to be part of a *ménage à trois*, some weird, alien sharing arrangement!

'No,' she finally managed to say. 'No!'

Freyn's eyes turned to ice. He looked at her, his glass still raised, and it was like being stared at by a vicious dog.

'Why not?'

Riley held her own glass, crushing it in her fingers, and tried to find the words.

'I ... well ... I just can't, that's all.' Lord, what a vague answer, she thought, but for the life of her she couldn't do better.

'What do you mean, you *can't*? You already *have*, or have you managed to forget that? Is it your reputation you're worried about? Truly? Because of course you know your friend Bill Gunn has already destroyed that?'

'That wouldn't surprise me; but it's not exactly my reputation,' she replied, fighting to find the right words. 'It's ... well ... I just can't share. I won't!'

Freyn stared in sullen silence, then she thought she noticed his lower lip twitch. Then again.

'So who asked you to?'

Riley was stuck for words. Did she dare admit to her spying at Battery Point? Did she dare question his involvement with Clarice Downs?

Freyn took the responsibility from her.

'I don't like to share either,' he said, 'but I've come to accept that I'll have to. Because I can't see you giving up your career just for me.

'Although,' and now his voice was full of authority, 'I'm damned if I'll have you riding that bulldozer once you're pregnant. No way! You can be a forester and a wife and a mother, but not all at the same time.'

Riley sat stunned. What ... what was he talking about? Pregnant? Suddenly the possibility struck her, though she hadn't even thought of it before.

But ... wife?

'Don't you think Clarice Downs might have some-thing to say about that?' she retorted unthinkingly. 'Or did you intend to keep both a wife and a mistress?'

'What the . . .?'

Then Freyn's hands were on her shoulders, pulling her to her feet, crushing her against him so tightly that the soft flannel shirt might not have existed.

'You,' he said after a kiss that scorched her lips, seared her very soul, 'are a very, very stupid woman.'

Then he frowned. 'Or else . . .'

He thrust her away to arms' length, captured her eyes with his stare. 'Has she been talking to you, trying to stir up trouble?'

'No,' Riley replied. Then went quiet, not knowing what on earth to say.

'Just as well,' he growled, and from the look in his eyes, it boded ill for Clarice Downs, or anybody else who dared oppose him, Riley thought.

'Just for the record, I haven't had anything much to do with Clarice since the first time I met you,' he said. 'Since the very first time.'

Now it was Riley's turn to raise an eyebrow, and she did. She couldn't help it, despite every other part of her body revelling in the wondrous warmth of being held so close to him.

'Oh, I don't deny taking her to Coles Bay,' he said without a whisker of guilt. 'But you, yourself, know how long that lasted. I just . . . couldn't be bothered, if that makes any sense. You killed it with the truth, made it seem all cheap and shoddy and . . . well, there wasn't any future in it, anyway.'

Riley said nothing; what could she say?

But he knew, knew there was something yet to be discovered, something she must bring into the open.

'What is it?' he said, and his voice was a whisper now, a compelling, hypnotic whisper she couldn't ignore, couldn't disobey.

'I . . . I saw her,' she began tentatively, 'coming out of

your apartment. With ... with your laundry.'

'Did you indeed?' His voice was full of disbelief. 'I do my own laundry, not that I can imagine Clarice doing it anyway; that's hardly her style!'

Riley remained obdurate; she knew what she had seen.

'I saw her coming out of your building with laundry, and it was men's laundry ... *your* laundry,' she insisted.

He laughed, then. Laughed, and took her into his arms for another kiss, this one more gentle and yet more insistent than the one before.

'Aha! Caught you on that one,' he cried with obvious delight. 'Because you didn't know—don't know, do you?—that Clarice lives in the same building, with her father. And *his* laundry she does do. Not mine!'

Whereupon he kissed her again, this time using his lips to explore her mouth, to sense the lack of conviction, the confusion that was sufficient to make her vulnerable.

'Hear me, Riley Jones,' he said, in a voice that was like doom, but doom with a warm heart. 'Hear me and don't you ever forget this. I have not touched Clarice Downs, nor any other woman, since the very first time we met. The first time! There in Centrepoint car park, and don't you forget that!

'I've enjoyed myself in the past, and I don't deny it,' he continued between kisses, 'but since the very first time I saw you, there was no other woman for me. Especially when it turned out the very next day that I could actually find out who you were, where to find you. I shudder to think of how difficult it might have been otherwise, but I'd have managed somehow.'

Riley could only stare at him. Was this the super-cool, super-sophisticated Freyn Devereux she knew? In his eyes was a wild light; his words tumbled out, heedless of consequence, heedless of his usual need for total control.

'It's too late now,' he was saying.

'Too late for what?'

'Too late for you to get away. I've got you here now, and by heaven, you're not getting away until I've said what I have to say. I'll get some sense into you if I have to pound it in with a sledge-hammer.'

'It would be much more logical if you'd just try making some sense yourself,' Riley replied, snuggling into his arms and positively revelling in the feeling.

He had said 'wife', she remembered. And he had meant it, which was more important, which was everything.

Now he said the rest, although hardly in the most romantic fashion possible.

'You will agree to marry me, and do it as soon as possible,' he whispered between delicious nibbles at her ear-lobe.

'And if I don't?'

She couldn't resist saying that. Couldn't resist just for the joy of knowing what his reply would be.

'If you don't agree, then Julius and his crew will arrive in the morning to find your clothes out in the paddock and you, my love, compromised to the point where you'll have no *choice* but to marry me.'

Now his lips were tracing lines of ecstasy down her throat, and his hands were inside the soft flannel of the shirt, making forays of their own along the softness of her skin. Riley shivered with pure delight.

'You're awfully sure of yourself,' she murmured between kisses.

'If I was sure of myself, I wouldn't have gone to so much trouble to make sure you couldn't escape,' he said, lifting his head once more to meet her eyes. 'Although I certainly hadn't planned on finding you quite so susceptible; it seems Mother Nature's on my side, too.'

Releasing her, though not without first making sure she was properly balanced and wouldn't fall, he stalked across the room to where he had hung up his suit coat. One hand plunged into a pocket, and when he returned to Riley it was outstretched to reveal an emerald ring that flashed green fire at every step.

'Not the traditional engagement ring, but it's going to be such a short engagement that it shouldn't matter,' he said. 'And besides, you're not what I'd call a traditional girl; you're so unique I spend half my time trying to figure you out.'

'And the other half confusing me,' Riley smiled. 'Are you honestly certain you know what you're doing?'

'I know that I love you; I think that you love me; and I'm damned if I'm going to spend any more time arguing and fighting to see who's going to admit it first,' he replied seriously.

'I've been carrying this ring around since before we left for Launceston, and you'd have been wearing it by now if you hadn't gone so ... strange that last morning.'

He reached out to take her hand, fitted the ring in place, then raised her fingers and kissed them as if to seal the bargain.

'I may kill young Gunn,' he growled. 'Because I'm sure it was his meddling that put a hex on everything by throwing your conscience into overdrive.'

'I thought ... I thought you might have believed what he said,' Riley faltered, and took immense delight in the laugh that comment provoked.

'I wouldn't have believed him if he'd told me the sun rose in the east,' Freyn chuckled. 'He was so obviously jealous.'

Then he kissed her again, and once more his fingers danced tunes of rapture across her skin.

Riley clasped her hands behind his neck, holding him against her as she returned his kisses with increasing ardour. Forgotten was the agony of Bill Gunn's meddling, the existence of Clarice Downs or any other woman in Freyn's past. All that mattered was *now*, now and the time to come.

The flannel shirt fell open, and his eyes and hands and lips were there to confirm the pleasure her body gave him, would give him.

'You are just so beautiful,' he whispered.

Then he picked her up, cradling her in his arms, and Riley didn't object to being carried this time as he shouldered his way through into the cottage's single, large bedroom.

'This is the end of the line,' he said. 'If you don't agree immediately to marry me as soon as possible, I won't be responsible for my actions.'

He laid her on the bed and began removing his shirt. Riley watched silently as his deft fingers slowly opened the buttons, her eyes drinking in the muscular body that was revealed.

'This is all so sudden,' she said then with a mischievous smile. 'I just can't make up my mind that quickly.'

Freyn's fingers paused at his belt buckle, then his own smile widened to match hers as he continued undressing.

'You leave me no choice then,' he said with a sudden fierce scowl. 'I'll just have to persuade you, and that means using any advantage I can.'

Riley glanced down at her bandaged ankle, then back to the muscular figure hovering over her.

'Would you take advantage of a poor, wounded girl?' she cried in mock horror.

'I would, and I will,' he replied, deftly slipping the flannel shirt from her shoulders. 'But you can think of it as my having regard for your health. You shouldn't be trying to walk on that ankle anyway.'

Then he was beside her, and walking was the furthest thing from her mind.

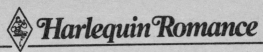# Harlequin Romance

Coming Next Month

2857 A MAN OF CONTRASTS Claudia Jameson
All signs point to a successful union when business owner
Elaine marries a widower with a small son. When she becomes
convinced he's still in love with his first wife, she faces the
future with dismay!

2858 KING OF THE HILL Emma Goldrick
Marcie regards the Adirondacks mountain cabin she inherited
as a needed resting place, until she becomes involved in a
family feud started by her late uncle. Even worse, she fights
with the one man she could love.

2859 VOYAGE OF DISCOVERY Hilda Nickson
Tha Canary Islands cruise is a new experience for Gail—a
pleasant shipboard romance would top it off. But falling in
love is a waste of time when the man in mind is not only
uninterested but engaged!

2860 THE LOVE ARTIST Valerie Parv
Carrie sees famous cartoonist Roger as fancy-free and
irresponsible, just like her father, who'd abandoned his family
to pursue art. No way will she consider Roger as a husband.

2861 RELATIVE STRANGERS Jessica Steele
Zarah travels to Norway to unravel the mystery surrounding
her real mother. She is shocked when she is regarded as a gold
digger even by the one man she can turn to for help—and love.

2862 LOVE UPON THE WIND Sally Stewart
Jenny's quiet London life is disrupted when her lawyer boss's
divorced son asks her to be his secretary. His second request is
even more shattering—to be the wife he needs as a respectable
candidate for Parliament!

Available in August wherever paperback books are sold, or
through Harlequin Reader Service.

In the U.S.
901 Fuhrmann Blvd.
P.O. Box 1397
Buffalo, N.Y. 14240-1397

In Canada
P.O. Box 603
Fort Erie, Ontario
L2A 5X3

Sarah

MAURA SEGER

Sarah wanted desperately to escape the clutches of her cruel father.
Philip needed a mother for his son, a mistress for his plantation.
It was a marriage of convenience.
Then it happened. The love they had tried to deny suddenly became a
blissful reality... only to be challenged by life's hardships and brutal
misfortunes.

Take 4 best-selling love stories FREE
Plus get a FREE surprise gift!

In August
Harlequin celebrates

The 1000th

Presents

Passionate Relationship

by
Penny Jordan

Harlequin Presents,
still and always the No. 1 romance
series in the world!